MISTLETOE AND KISSES

A Duke of Strathmore Holiday Novella

SASHA COTTMAN

Also by Sasha Cottman

The Duke of Strathmore

Letter from a Rake (ebook, print, audio)

An Unsuitable Match (ebook, print, audio)

The Duke's Daughter (ebook, print, audio)

A Scottish Duke for Christmas (ebook, print)

My Gentleman Spy (ebook, print, audio)

Lord of Mischief (ebook, print, audio)

The Ice Queen (ebook, print, audio)

Two of a Kind (ebook, print, audio)

Mistletoe & Kisses (ebook, print)

Regency Rockstars

Reid (ebook, print)

Owen (ebook, print)

Callum (ebook, print)

Kendal (ebook, print)

London Lords

An Italian Count for Christmas (ebook, print)

Chapter One

C ambridge, December 1790

Lord Hugh Radley closed his travel trunk one last time, silently reassuring himself that he had indeed got everything he would need for the trip to Scotland. He turned and groaned. There, sitting on the end of his bed, was the pair of boots he was certain he had already packed.

"You would forget your head if it wasn't attached," he muttered.

He would be needing the boots for the ice-covered roads around his family home in Scotland. After adding the boots and closing the lid of the travel trunk once more, he stepped back and allowed the porters to take his luggage.

He had been looking forward to this day for months. Christmas at the Radley clan's ancestral home, Strathmore Castle, was always a special time. Hugh was champing at the bit to see his family.

He would be making the trip north this year, along with two of his sisters and their respective spouses. With all of them in the one coach, it was going to be a cramped four-day journey. He had packed several books in his travel bag, intending to bury his nose in them rather than attempt hours of small talk. As much as he loved his family, he had important documents he needed to study and commit to memory before he returned to England in the new year.

"When the coach arrives, could you make sure my luggage is safely loaded onto it? If my family asks, please tell them I have to see a friend before I leave, but I won't be long." He followed the porters out of his private rooms and locked the door behind him.

For a moment, he stood with the palm of his hand laid against the solid oak door. It would be the last time he touched it. He was no longer a student at St John's College, Cambridge University. His days of living on the campus of the hallowed halls of learning were now at an end.

"Lord Hugh Radley, BA Theology. Fancy that," he said.

He crossed the college courtyard then strolled along a walkway with edges bordered by tall white rose bushes before finally arriving at a black door with a brass nameplate.

Professor J. L. Gray.

He knocked on the door and opened it. Professor Gray's rooms were never locked.

"Mary, it's Hugh. I've come to say farewell," he cheerfully called out.

A hand rose from behind a pile of old exam papers and waved. "Down here."

Stepping around a neat stack of books, he found her. Mary Gray was kneeling on the floor, dust pan and brush in hand.

"What are you doing?" he asked.

"A spot of cleaning. I moved a few more of Papa's piles of papers this morning and actually found the floor. I dread to think the last time the stone flagging saw daylight," she replied.

He held a hand out to her and helped Mary to her feet. Her gaze took in his coat and scarf, and she smiled.

"So, you are off to Scotland for Christmas?

"Yes, the travel coach will be here shortly. I have sent the porters and my luggage out to the main courtyard to await its arrival," he replied.

She looked around the room, then back to him. "It must feel a little odd to be leaving here for the last time."

He had thought it would be his last time, but earlier in the week he had been given the news that he still had some minor studies to complete before he could take up his post as curate at St Martins-in-the-Fields in central London.

"Actually, it's not the *very* last time I shall be on campus. I have to come back after Christmas for a week. I will stay at one of the inns in town, but I shall drop by and say hello," he replied.

Mary nodded, a tight smile sat briefly on her lips. She picked up another pile of papers and straightened them. He sensed she was nervous.

"Is your sister Adelaide making the trip with her newborn? I remember when she visited at half term and she was complaining about how swollen her ankles were," said Mary. She put the papers down again and stood, tapping her fingers on the top of the pile.

Mary always fidgeted when she was uncomfortable about something.

Adelaide and Charles Alexandre had been blessed with the birth of a son, William, in early October. Hugh was dreading the prospect of sharing a cramped travel coach with a wailing infant but needs must.

"Yes, she is. My brother, Ewan, has commanded that as many members of the family as possible should make the trip this year. My sister Anne and her new husband, the Duke of Mowbray, are also going to be travelling with us," he said. His other sister Davina, the Countess of Shale, was with child and unable to travel.

Mary wiped her hands on her apron. "Do you have time for a cup of coffee before you go?"

Hugh shook his head. "No. The coach will be here soon, and I shouldn't keep them waiting. I just wanted to come by and wish you a merry Christmas."

At his words, her face lit up. She quickly scuttled from the room, then returned with a small parcel in her hands. She offered it to Hugh. He set down his travel bag, along with the book he was carrying, and took it.

"Merry Christmas, Hugh. It's not much; just a little gift," she said.

He accepted the present with a sinking feeling in the pit of his stomach. He had been so disorganized and muddleheaded when it came to making ready for the journey to Scotland that he had completely forgotten to buy her a Christmas present.

Poor form, Radley. Too busy thinking about yourself, and not enough about her.

With the death of her father earlier in the year, Mary would be spending her first Christmas without her beloved papa. Hugh felt the heat of embarrassment burning on his cheeks. "Oh, I am so sorry. I completely forgot to get you a gift. I am the very worst of friends," he said.

She nodded at the parcel in his hands. "That's perfectly alright. You have been busy studying. Christmas no doubt crept up on you," she replied.

Hugh opened the present and his discomfort deepened. Inside was a bar of beautifully wrapped French soap, and a small bottle of gentleman's cologne. It must have cost Mary a good deal of money. Money, he suspected she did not have in abundance.

"You shouldn't have," he said.

She smiled. "Nonsense. As soon as I saw them in the shop, I thought of you. I hope you like them."

"I do, and I promise I shall bring you back a special gift from Scotland when I return after Christmas. I cannot believe that I could be so absentminded to forget about getting you something. I am mortified," he replied.

Mary reached out and placed a hand on Hugh's cheek. "It's fine. The fact that you like my present is reward enough."

The warmth of her hand on his face stirred once more to life the longing he had held for her these past two years. Somewhere in the endless nights of her bringing him toast and coffee for supper while he studied alongside her father, his thoughts of Mary had changed from those of friendship to those of love.

But with her father being the head of theology and divinity, and the man directly responsible for the conferring of Hugh's degree, he had not dared to move on those feelings.

Now, the temptation to pull her into his arms and kiss her senseless was almost too strong to resist. The heavenly scent of her perfume filled his senses. His fingers twitched with anticipation.

When she withdrew her hand and turned away, Hugh was left to battle emotions of regret and relief. She had never shown any sign of being interested in him in a romantic way, so it was best that he not act on those impulses. With her father now gone, only a cad of the lowest kind would press his attentions on a vulnerable young woman.

"So, when are you leaving to visit with your mother's family?" he asked. He prayed she did not hear the shake in his voice as he spoke.

"Oh, sometime later in the week. I am yet to make final arrangements," she replied.

"And you will be back after the new year? I only ask because when I return, I would like for us to have a conversation."

A conversation that he hoped would involve him declaring his love for her, and Mary, in turn, considering that a future shared with him might not be the worst thing she could imagine doing with her life.

A knock at the door interrupted them, but as he turned away, Hugh caught a glimpse of Mary. She was biting down on her bottom lip.

It stopped him in his tracks.

Chapter Two

"We thought we might find you here. Hello Mary."

Hugh's sister Adelaide and her husband, Charles, stepped through the doorway. Charles's held a small bundle in his arms—a bundle which was making gurgling and snuffling sounds.

"Did the porter manage to get my luggage to the coach?" asked Hugh, stirring from his thoughts of Mary.

Adelaide snorted. "And hello to you too, dearest brother."

Mary stifled a grin. For all his intelligence, Hugh Radley was at times a tad clueless when it came to social situations. His oversight in having not gotten her a Christmas present was so very typical of Hugh.

She understood it, and was sure to forgive him, but it still hurt. The private moment they had shared when she'd touched his face meant more to her than any shop-bought gift could. He had leaned in toward her, and for the briefest of moments she'd imagined he was about to kiss her.

Yet again, her hopes for Hugh to see her as more than just a friend had vanished like the morning mist.

He is the son of a duke, and you are merely the daughter of a deceased university professor. Hugh Radley would never think to love someone like you, let alone marry her.

"Hello Adelaide. How was the trip up from London?" said Mary.

Adelaide stepped past her brother, giving him a small disapproving shake of the head. She greeted Mary with a hug. "Good. William slept most of the way. We also got a good night's sleep at the inn where we stopped in Sandy last night. We should all pray that he keeps this up for the rest of the journey north," she replied.

Hugh turned to Charles. "Where are Anne and Mowbray?"

Charles and Adelaide exchanged a look. Baby Will stirred in his father's arms, and Adelaide hurried over to him.

"I think it is time for your morning feed. Mary, do you have a chair or somewhere that I can nurse Will?" she asked.

Mary pointed to the doorway of her father's old study. "There is a comfortable rocking chair in the corner if you wish."

Adelaide took Will from his father, and Mary ushered them into the room. In between scattered piles of books and papers, the room also somehow managed to hold the chair and a large desk. Until recent days, the desk had been buried under a pile of midterm papers her father had succeeded in marking before his sudden passing. Mary had managed to clear the papers away earlier in the week, and like the floor in the front room, the top of the desk now saw the light of day.

While Adelaide settled into the chair and allowed Will to latch on, Mary took a seat behind her father's desk and sat with her hands gently clasped.

"I am sorry about your father," said Adelaide.

"Thank you. And thank you for the lovely letter you sent. I appreciated it greatly," replied Mary.

Adelaide Alexandre, nee Radley, had always made a point of calling in to see Mary and her father whenever she was visiting her brother. For a duke's daughter, Adelaide had a surprisingly pleasant affinity with people across all social classes.

"May I ask what you are doing for Christmas? Are you staying here alone at the college? It would be a terrible pity if you were," Adelaide said.

Mary tightened her fingers together. Thankfully she had shown

Adelaide into the study, rather than her bedroom. There was little evidence in this room that she was about to vacate the apartment for good.

"I am due to visit with family for Christmas. I am just waiting for their letter to confirm the arrangements," she replied, holding onto the lie she had already given to Hugh.

Will began to fuss, and it was to Mary's relief that Adelaide became too distracted with breastfeeding her son to press for further details of her family.

"Could I offer you a cup of tea?" Mary asked.

"Thank you, Mary, that would be lovely. Though we can't stay long; Charles wants to make good time once we leave Cambridge. The road through to Stilton might be difficult in the fading light if we leave too late," replied Adelaide.

Mary looked at William and immediately understood Charles' concerns. The last thing any new parent wanted was to find themselves stuck in a carriage late at night with a tired and hungry infant.

After their final farewells to Mary, Hugh and the Alexandre family climbed aboard the travel coach. Hugh pulled down the window and waved to Mary as she stood on the side of the street. It was only when she was finally lost from sight that he drew up the glass and sat back in his seat.

"So why did Anne and Mowbray cry off from coming to Scotland?" he asked.

He hadn't thought it polite to press for further details about the obvious absence of his sister and her husband, Clifford, the Duke of Mowbray, in front of Mary.

Charles rolled his eyes. "They are not coming for Christmas. And for that we should all be truly grateful."

Adelaide kissed her baby son on the forehead and cooed. "Your uncle is not coming because he says he is a *bloody* duke, with his own *bloody* castle, and he does not see why he should have to travel all the way to *bloody* Scotland for Christmas. Isn't that right, my beautiful boy?"

"If the first word that our son speaks is *bloody*, I shall blame Mowbray. I cannot deny that I am glad he is not coming for Christmas," replied Charles.

Hugh was not the least surprised that Anne and Mowbray were not making the trip. In the short time that they had been married, the Duke and Duchess of Mowbray had established themselves as being in a near-constant state of war with one another. When they were not going into battle, they were being sickeningly sweet to each other. Having witnessed both forms of behavior in the newlyweds, Hugh was not completely certain which one he disliked the most.

He was ashamed to be relieved that Anne and Mowbray were not making the journey with them, but he knew he shared Charles's sentiments.

"Oh well, that leaves more room for us in the coach." He could now spread out his study papers and books without fear of getting an elbow in the ribs from the Duke of Mowbray.

Chapter Three

Mary walked back to her rooms and closed the door behind her. She had watched the coach until it had disappeared from sight, crushed by the knowledge that it would be the last time she would ever see Hugh leave the cramped but homely rooms at St John's College, which she and her father had always called home.

She wiped a tear away, gritting her teeth to force back any others that may have threatened. Crying would not change her circumstances, and she knew from many bitter, lonely nights that it would not bring her father back. She was now on her own in the world.

She had cleaned the main room from top to bottom over the past few days, intending that the new tenant should have a fresh start when they arrived early in the new year. Never would she have it said that the rooms had been left in anything but workable condition. Her father's valuable papers and books she would entrust to the next head of theology and divinity. His clothes had been gratefully received by the head grounds keeper who promised to find each item a suitable new home.

In her tiny bedroom, she squeezed between the wall and her single bed. The linen was freshly laundered, and the mattress had been hung out in the late afternoon sun the previous day to air. On top of the small nightstand was a travel bag, and next to it, her long red wool coat.

Picking up the coat, she put it on and buttoned it all the way to the neck. The first snow had fallen in the previous week, and the air outside was icy.

Travel bag in hand, she stepped out of her bedroom before glancing back one last time. She would never sleep in this room again. It was another final goodbye.

"Come on, Mary. If you keep this up, you will be here all day. You cannot say farewell to every single room and object," she muttered.

She indulged in one final tour of the apartment. She had cleaned her father's study earlier in the week, and shed a million tears as she did so, grateful that Hugh had been too busy to visit that day.

Hugh.

He had been her father's star pupil. A man destined for greatness in the Church of England, perhaps someday even becoming the Archbishop of Canterbury. With the Duke of Strathmore as his older brother, Hugh Radley had enough connections and talent to make that a reality.

Mary set her bag down and then collected the empty cups and plates from where her visitors had left them, taking them over to the washbowl near the fire. After washing and drying them, she carefully placed them on a nearby shelf.

For some inexplicable reason she left Hugh's cup for last. She washed it in the warm soapy water, and then held it. She pretended to herself that it was still warm from when Hugh had last touched it. She raised it to her lips and kissed the cup where she knew his lips had been.

So close, yet so far away.

It was a simple coffee cup with a red, gold, and blue mosaic pattern on white china. It was a one-of-a-kind in her home. Nearly every day for the past two and a half years she had made Hugh a cup of coffee in it and brought it to him as he studied late into the night.

Mary chuckled softly. Hugh liked his coffee thick and mud-like. No sugar, and just a dash of milk. The cup would sit untouched for hours while Hugh and her father engaged in long philosophical discussions, often only being finally drained when the coffee had long gone cold.

Opening her bag, she pulled out a woolen scarf and wrapped it around the cup. She would keep it as a memento of all those wonderful days.

When Hugh returned to Cambridge after Christmas, she would meet him somewhere else in the town and patiently wait for him to tell her of his exciting plans for the future. She would share the news of her own changed circumstances as a mere afterthought, something to be noted and then never mentioned again.

She carefully placed the cup into her bag. Then with one final tearful look, she bid farewell to the only home she had ever known. "Time to go, Mary Gray. Time to put the past behind you."

She closed the door of the rooms for the last time and locked it. After returning the key to the groundkeeper's office, she crossed over the cloisters and headed toward the main entrance of St John's College. It took all her willpower not to look back, not to cry.

Thank God Hugh was not there to see her leave.

Chapter Four

"Oh, blast," muttered Hugh.

He put his hand back into his travel bag one more time and rummaged around, but his prayers were not answered. The book was nowhere to be found. He had already emptied and repacked his leather satchel twice in his desperate search; the travel bag had been his last hope. He slumped back on the bench and huffed with frustration. Yet again, he had misplaced something.

"What's the matter?" asked Adelaide. She held a sleeping William in her arms, the infant having dozed off after his mother had fed him at the college.

Charles held out his hands and took his son from her. Will did not stir as his father tucked him into the crook of his arm.

"I had a book on ecclesiastical law that I needed to study while I was in Scotland. I must have left it behind in my room," Hugh replied.

"If it is important, could you perhaps secure a copy in Edinburgh?" asked Charles.

Hugh shook his head. "It's a Church of England lawbook. Edinburgh comes under the Church of Scotland. I doubt very much if I would be able to find a copy in Edinburgh. I'm sorry to have to ask this of you both, but I need that book."

Adelaide gave him a sisterly, knowing look. Hugh had a long history of losing things, finding them again, and then losing them once more.

"Well at least we are not far from Cambridge. It won't take us too long to return and collect it," replied Adelaide.

Charles covered his son's ears as Hugh stood and rapped on the roof of the coach. To the relief of all, the sleeping Will did not stir. After giving quick instructions to the driver, Hugh sat down in his seat and gave a sigh of relief as the coach made a turn in the road and headed back toward Cambridge.

"I think I know exactly where I left it. I swear I picked it up three times this morning, intending to put it in my bag," he eventually said.

He raked his fingers through his hair, frustrated and a little more than angry with himself. He had set the book down when Mary had given him the Christmas gift. The book was still on top of a pile of marked exam papers in Professor Gray's old rooms.

Once they reached St John's College, Hugh jumped down from the coach. "I won't be long. I shall say a brief, polite hello and goodbye again to Mary, then be back."

He hurried across the grounds, through the cloisters, and with a quick knock on the door, took hold of the handle.

The handle did not budge. He rattled it several times, thinking it must be stuck. When it finally dawned on him that the door was indeed locked, he frowned. The Grays rarely, if ever, locked their door.

"Mary!" he called out. Where on earth could she have gone? He needed that book.

"Lord Radley?"

He turned and when he caught sight of one of the college groundskeepers, he could have cried.

"Please tell me you have your set of keys upon your person; I need to access Professor Gray's rooms," he said.

The groundskeeper scowled. No groundskeeper worth his salt would be wandering the university grounds without his master set of keys. "Of course, I have my keys. Though they are no longer Professor Gray's rooms," replied the man.

Hugh nodded. He was in too much of a hurry to discuss the passing of his old professor. In his mind, as long as Mary remained in residence, they would always be Professor Gray's rooms.

The groundskeeper unlocked the door, then, after promising to come back and lock it again once Hugh was gone, he took his leave.

Hugh hurried into the room, sighing with relief as he spotted his book.

"Thank heavens for that," he muttered, as he picked it up.

He paused for a moment; something in the room was different. He looked at the piles of books and papers. They were stacked and arranged neater than he had ever seen them. He had not noticed the changes when he had been here earlier with Mary, his interest focused on her. He slowly took in the rest of the room.

Papers which were normally haphazardly thrown together had been put into neat bundles and tied off with string. The bookshelves were now full. Mary had made mention of having been cleaning, but until this moment, Hugh had not thought to ask why. The professor had always liked the messy look of his rooms, and Mary had sworn to keep them exactly as he had left them for at least the first year after his passing.

He poked his head inside Professor Gray's old study and was surprised to be greeted with the sight of a tidy room. Hugh had never seen the top of the professor's desk before. The sight was disconcerting.

Now that is odd. What have you been doing, Mary?

He steeled himself as he opened Mary's bedroom door. He was invading her privacy, but his concerns held his mind. As he saw the bedding which had been folded and put to one side, a rising sense of panic gripped him. The cupboard where her clothes should hang was empty.

"Calm down, Radley. She has just been getting things ship-shape before leaving to visit her mother's family," he told himself.

His words, however, were cold comfort. Not more than an hour ago, Mary had told him she had not had confirmation of her visit from her relatives. Yet she had clearly gone somewhere and taken all of her possessions with her.

Stepping back into the main room, he found the groundskeeper waiting. "Did you find what you were looking for, my lord?"

Hugh frowned. He barely noticed the book in his hand.

"Yes and no," he replied.

"It's a pity about the Professor and Miss Gray. They were always kind to the staff around here," said the groundskeeper.

Hugh tightened his hold on the book. "What do you mean?"

"Not that it's my place, but it would have been nice if Miss Gray could have stayed on at the university for a little while longer. But I suppose they needed the rooms for the new professor, and she had to go." The groundskeeper nervously jangled the ring of keys he held in his hand. University staff were meant to be seen and not heard.

Cold, hard realization settled heavily on Hugh's shoulders. Mary was not visiting relatives; she had left St John's College for good. And she hadn't told him.

Think. Think what to do.

He rallied his thoughts. "You wouldn't by any chance know where Miss Gray has gone, would you?" he asked.

The groundskeeper shook his head. "Not exactly. Though, she did make mention that she had found a room in a boarding house not far from the market square when she visited the office just before she left."

"How long ago did she leave?"

"Not a quarter of the hour ago, I would say. She may not have got that far from the college grounds," replied the groundskeeper.

After slipping the man a coin and wishing him a merry Christmas, Hugh raced outside and to the waiting travel coach. He flung open the door.

"They have thrown Mary out!" he cried.

Adelaide's eyes grew wide. It took an instant for Hugh to realize that it wasn't so much about his revelation, as the volume at which he had delivered it. Charles put a finger to his lips. William stirred in his sleep and let out a soft whimper.

Everyone held their breaths. To the relief of all, William remained asleep.

"What do you mean?" replied Charles quietly.

Hugh caught the attention of the coach driver and issued brief instructions. He then climbed aboard and closed the door.

"The university needed the rooms for the new professor, and Mary has had to vacate them. One of the groundskeepers told me Mary left only a short while ago. I've asked the coach driver to head down toward the market square and see if we can spot her," he explained.

Charles took up a position on one side of the coach, while Hugh sat at the other window. He dropped the glass window down and poked his head outside.

"Where are you?" he muttered.

As the coach entered Bridge Street, it slowed to a crawl. Being the week before Christmas, everyone was out in the town center. And all, it would appear, were headed toward Cambridge Market Square. Hugh snarled his frustration. They would never find Mary in this crush of carriages and people.

He rapped on the roof of the coach and instructed the driver to pull over to the side of the street.

"What are you doing?" asked Charles.

"If you keep going and continue to look out on the other side of the street, I will see if I can make headway on foot. Just remember she will be wearing red," Hugh replied.

He hurried away from the coach, frantically looking for any sign of a red coat and Mary. He was met with a sea of black, brown, and gray. Breaking into a run, he slipped between the gaps of other pedestrians as he fought to make his way through the Christmas crowds.

He had gone only a few yards before a hand thumped him on the back. Turning, he found a breathless Charles standing before him.

"She is on the other side, fifty yards on."

Hugh nodded his thanks and made a mad dash across the street. He narrowly avoided being run over by a heavily laden mail coach which was travelling in the other direction.

His reckless pursuit, however, was immediately rewarded with the sight of Mary's red coat as she turned into Market Street.

"Mary!"

She kept walking. Hugh broke into a full run, grabbing hold of the back of her coat when he finally caught up.

"Mary, didn't you hear me?"

She turned, and as their gazes met a look of shock appeared on her face. She was clearly not expecting to see him.

"Hugh? What . . . what are you doing here?" she stammered.

"I forgot a book . . . I mean, what are you doing *here*?! Why didn't you tell me you had been evicted?" His relief at finding her was quickly replaced with the anger he had managed to keep at bay since discovering the truth of her deception. He continued to hold fast to her coat.

Her head and shoulders dropped. "I was going to tell you, but with everything else happening in your life, it didn't seem important."

He released his grip on her coat and stood staring at her. "How could you not think you were important to me?"

Chapter Five

Mary's heart sank. She had been waiting patiently for weeks until Hugh had left for Scotland so she could quietly pack her things and leave the university. Her earlier relief at his departure was now crushed by seeing him standing before her. The look of angry disappointment on his face added to her woes.

She had hoped to avoid this conversation until after Christmas, because knowing Hugh and his ingrained sense of justice, she had a strong inkling as to how he would react to the news that she was now living in a boarding house.

She straightened her back and steeled herself for the inevitable conversation. "I have taken a room at number sixty-two Market Street, and I plan to tutor students from there during each college term," she replied, nodding toward the green door of her new lodgings.

His eyes narrowed. She could almost hear his brain processing her words. When he looked at the bag containing all her worldly goods which she clutched in her hands, Mary held her breath.

"But they threw you out? Put you on the street without a thought for your future? he said.

"Not in so many words, but yes, I was asked to vacate the rooms.

The new professor will be coming sometime after Christmas," she replied.

Hugh's face darkened. "Your father gave the university thirty-three years of faithful service, and yet they cannot even see their way to allow his daughter to remain in the only home she has ever known. And to top it all off, it is Christmas!" he said.

Mary sensed one of Hugh's rants about the spirit of Christmas and the true meaning of the holy celebration was imminent. When she saw Charles Alexandre climb down from the coach, holding his infant son in his arms, she almost cheered. No matter how angry he was, Hugh would not dare make a scene in public, and especially not in front of his family.

She was wrong.

Hugh immediately turned to his brother in law. "Do you know what those cads at the university have done, the week before Christmas?" he said.

Charles looked from Hugh to Mary, then down at his sleeping son. He stopped and kept his distance a yard or so away.

"They have thrown her out!" bellowed Hugh.

Charles took a step back. "Yes, you had already mentioned that. I might just leave this to my wife."

Charles retreated back toward the peaceful sanctuary of the coach. Adelaide's head appeared in the doorway and the couple exchanged a few brief words. Even from where she stood, Mary could see that the news of her changed abode had not been well received. Bless the Radley family and their need to preserve the sanctity of Christmas.

Adelaide hurried down from the coach and marched over to where Hugh and Mary stood.

"Is it true? They have evicted you?" asked Adelaide.

Mary lifted her travel bag and held it close against her stomach. Hugh and Adelaide were her friends, but even as they both rose in her defense, she felt the need for protection. "Yes. No. I mean. Oh."

If she didn't take the heat out of the moment, the pot was about to boil over. She had a vivid image of both Hugh and Adelaide marching up to the faculty dean and giving him a piece of their collective mind.

Charles and Will would no doubt be pressganged into service to support the cause.

Mary took a deep breath and summoned her courage. The last thing she needed was for the Radley siblings to stir up a fight with the head of the school whose students she was relying upon to make her future living.

"They asked me to vacate some months ago. I dillydallied about it until they were forced to send me a second letter earlier this month. It is all my fault I am having to make the change so close to Christmas," she said.

The truth was, she had ignored much of what had happened during the year; her father's sudden passing left her numb to nearly everything other than the absolute necessities of marking overflow exam papers, some sleep, and bringing Hugh his supper each night. She had not had the strength to consider leaving the only home she had ever known. To know that she would no longer be counted as a member of the university family was beyond her grief-clouded mind.

Adelaide, bless her, was having none of it. While Hugh seemed to have calmed down a notch, his sister was just getting riled up.

"So, what you are saying is that you will be spending Christmas alone in a boarding house room with no family," said Adelaide.

Mary clutched the bag tighter to herself, suddenly feeling very alone in the world. She should have written to her mother's family in Devon and asked to visit for Christmas. Not that she actually knew them, but still, she chided herself for the oversight.

"Hugh, take Mary's travel bag. Mary, come with us and get into the coach. You are coming to Scotland. We will not allow you to spend Christmas on your own."

Words of feeble protest struggled to her lips, but when Mary saw Hugh's tight-set jaw as he stepped forward and took a hold of the bag, she knew they would be to no avail. She released her grip on the travel bag, giving him a wan smile as he tucked it under his arm.

"Good. That is settled. When we return after Christmas, I shall have a word with the dean," he said.

Mary followed Adelaide and Hugh back to the coach. As she took her seat inside, Charles leaned forward. "You weren't seriously thinking that they were going to let you spend Christmas on your own, were you? The Radley family's Christmas motto is that no one gets left behind."

"Unless of course you are a *bloody* stubborn duke," muttered Adelaide.

Chapter Six

❧

With Mary now on board the travel coach, and Hugh's missing book safely in his hands, they set out across country to meet the Great North Road and continue their journey to Scotland.

While Adelaide and Mary were making polite conversation about the baby and how well he was doing, Hugh was lost in his own thoughts, most of which consisted of him raging at himself. By the time they made their final stop for the day at the Bell Inn in Stilton, he had worked himself into such a foul mood that he cried off supper and went for a long walk instead.

With his hands stuffed deep into the pockets of his greatcoat, he trudged through the snow-covered streets of the town. There were only so many ways a man could be angry with himself, but Hugh Radley was determined to work his way through the list. He passed several taverns on the road and was tempted to go inside and have a pint, but he knew he would need more than alcohol to take the edge off his self-loathing.

The walk finally began to have its desired effect and his mood lifted. As he turned and started to head back to the inn, his thoughts returned to Mary. It was a relief to know that she would not be spending Christmas on her own, that she was coming to Scotland with him. He had much to atone for when it came to her.

Mary had not only been dealing with grief over the death of her father, but the impending loss of her home. He, meanwhile, had been so preoccupied with his final exams and career progression that he had failed to see what was happening under his very nose. He had not been there for her when she needed a friend.

"And to top it all off, you forgot to get her a Christmas present. Hugh Radley you are a selfish blackguard," he muttered.

Back at the inn, he found Charles rugged up in a greatcoat and seated in front of an open fire outside in the rear mews, his back against the wall of the stables. His head was buried in a newspaper. He didn't look up until Hugh sat down beside him.

Hugh glanced at the newspaper. It was the *L'Ami du Peuple;* a radical popular newspaper from Paris. With the French king in custody, and the whole of France in turmoil, émigrés such as Charles were constantly in search of news from their homeland.

"What is happening in France?" asked Hugh.

Charles folded the paper up and sat it on his lap. While his hands remained steady, his boot was tapping hard on the stone ground. He sighed. "They have given all French citizens who are living abroad a deadline to return home or forfeit any land that they hold in France. I shall have to sell everything I own within the next twelve months or lose it all. I tell you, Hugh, France is going to hell."

For the second time that day, Hugh was sharply reminded that the world did not revolve around his studies or himself. Charles had been an open supporter of King Louis, but with the king and his family now under arrest, Charles dared not return home. His brother-in-law was trapped in exile in England.

Charles pulled two cheroots from his pocket and lit them using a lighted taper from the fire. He handed one to Hugh.

"I'm sorry, Charles. It must be so hard to be this close to home but know that you cannot risk going back."

"If it was only me, I might chance it, but I have a wife and a child to consider now. I would never put Adelaide through that sort of worry, knowing that I might never return. People have started disappearing in France, and I have a feeling that we are only just at the beginning of something terrible," he said.

Hugh drew back deeply on his cheroot, then held the smoke in his mouth for a moment before pushing it out with his tongue. A pale gray smoke ring formed and hung in the still night air. Charles snorted his appreciation of the trick.

"*Astuce*," he said.

Hugh settled back against the stone wall of the stables. It was good to be headed home to Scotland. He had missed Christmas the previous year, being too busy with exams and preparation for his last year at university, and he had spent the last twelve months regretting it.

"I hope you didn't mind Adelaide and I inviting Mary to come with us. We both got a little riled up over her having to find a new home after all those years living at the university," he said.

Charles was a decent man, his calm nature a balm to his wife's sometime skittish behavior. His sister had chosen her partner in life wisely.

"Is that what you are telling yourself? That the only reason you raced after Mary in the middle of Cambridge was out of some sense of righting an injustice? Please, let me know when you actually start to believe that *coq et taureau* story," replied Charles.

Hugh didn't answer. He could proclaim his actions were all in aid of a young woman unfairly treated, but they both knew there was more to it than that. He and Adelaide could have gone to speak with the dean before leaving Cambridge; matters could have been resolved. But that would have left Mary still in Cambridge, and he on the road to Scotland.

He drew back once more on the cheroot, silently grateful when Charles opened his newspaper once more and went back to reading.

Today had been a day of unexpected revelations. He'd experienced genuine fear when he discovered that Mary had been evicted from her home. Of greater concern was the fact that she had not confided in him. That she had decided her own overwhelming problems were too insignificant to share.

That she somehow thought he didn't care.

"How long are you planning to stay at Strathmore Castle?" asked Charles.

"Christmas, then Hogmanay, finally finishing up on Handsel Monday." Hugh counted the days out on his fingers. If they arrived on the twenty-third of December, then stayed to Handsel Monday on the seventeenth, he would have just under a month in Scotland.

He wanted to get back to England earlier, but knew his older brother, Ewan, would insist he stayed for the annual handing over of gifts to all the castle staff on Handsel Monday.

"I will be leaving early on the eighteenth of January," he replied.

Charles nodded. "Well, dear brother, you may think you have plenty of time in which to sort out the Mary Gray situation on your own. But I would counsel you to make haste if you want the decision to be yours alone."

Hugh understood the underlying meaning of his brother-in-law's words. The previous year, the dowager duchess, Lady Alison, and Great Aunt Maude had shamelessly played cupid. On Christmas Day, the Duke of Strathmore had made Lady Caroline Hastings his wife.

Knowing his mother and great aunt, as soon as they set eyes on Mary, they would be looking to replicate their success. Two Christmases; two weddings. He couldn't fault the logic. He wouldn't be disappointed if indeed that was what transpired, but only if Mary was willing to take a chance with her heart.

Hugh broke off the burning end of his cheroot, and after butting it out in a small patch of snow, he put the remainder in his coat pocket. He got to his feet.

"I shall bid you a good night, Charles," he said.

"I won't be long out here. Adelaide is settling William down, and I shall go up to our room shortly. Good night, Hugh."

Hugh snorted. Charles would do anything to avoid being exposed to the smell of his son's soiled linen clout before bedtime.

As he walked back into the inn and sought the warmth of his bed, Hugh Radley was struck with a thought. Earlier in the day he had sent prayers to heaven about finding his book and they had been answered. With the unexpected addition of Mary to the group headed for Scotland, perhaps another of his longtime entreaties had finally been heard.

Chapter Seven

Mary looked at the price tag on the long emerald and blue scarf and put it back on the table. It was beautifully made, the thread around its edges no doubt real gold. The silk scarf was worth more than the cost of all the clothes on her back.

"That's nice. It suits you—it matches your enchanting green eyes."

Mary saw the smile on Adelaide's face. Her remark about Mary's looks was the latest in a slowly growing list of small kind ones Adelaide had been offering since they'd left Cambridge.

Mary nodded, then turned to look at another shelf of goods in the shop.

They were in High Street, Edinburgh, along the Royal Mile, undertaking a morning of shopping before leaving on the last leg of their journey to Strathmore Castle.

Mary wasn't particularly interested in shopping; the small number of coins in her possession had all been earmarked for living expenses. She could not risk spending money on non-essential items until she had managed to secure a regular group of students in need of her tutoring. Building that client base, however, would take time. And in the meantime, she still needed to pay rent and feed herself.

Still, it was good to be out of the travel coach. Three days from Cambridge to Edinburgh in even a spacious coach, such as the one hired by Charles Alexandre, had played havoc with her back and hips.

Hugh had not helped matters either, constantly asking her how she was to survive going forward. Making lists of people he would speak to on her behalf at the college to get her old living quarters back. Then a shorter list of people he would speak to if his first overtures failed. By the time he had finished mentioning yet again that his brother was the Duke of Strathmore and his brother-in-law the Duke of Mowbray, Mary had developed a headache which lasted two whole days.

She quietly chided herself. At least she wasn't spending Christmas alone in the bedsit of a boarding house. Hugh and the Alexandres had no connection to her beyond mere friendship, and they were under no obligation to render her assistance. She should be grateful that they wanted to help at all.

"So where else do you have in mind to visit today?" asked Mary.

Adelaide shrugged. It was the first day she had let Charles take their son off her hands for more than an hour. Mary had noted that every so often, Adelaide would look down at her empty arms and sigh. She was missing her baby.

"We will be leaving early tomorrow for Strathmore Castle, so if you wish to walk the street at the bottom of Edinburgh Castle and wander into a few more shops, I can meet you back at the inn in time for supper. I have a private errand to undertake in the meantime; I have something to collect," replied Adelaide.

Having never visited Scotland before, Mary was keen to take in a few more of the sights of the great city of Edinburgh. There was every chance she may not get the opportunity again.

With Adelaide off on her secret mission, Mary was surprised as to how quickly she welcomed the time alone. The one thing she did not welcome, however, was the biting wind which pierced her coat. Cambridge was cold in winter, but a thick scarf and her trusty red coat had seen her through the worst of the chilly days. Here in Scotland, her English attire failed against the onslaught of an icy Scottish breeze. Standing outside a drapery, peering in through the window, she hugged herself in an effort to stay warm.

"Stockings—that is what I need. Thick wool ones," she muttered.

Hugh dropped the last of his Christmas gifts into his leather satchel and gave himself a silent cheer. "Ewan, Caroline, David, Mama, Great Aunt Maude, Adelaide, Charles, and William. Not that the baby will actually do anything with his gift, but it's the thought that counts," he said.

His Christmas shopping was complete. At the bottom of the satchel lay two other gifts. One was a special Christmas present for Mary, the other a small box.

It was the item inside the small box which had taken Hugh most of the morning to choose. He had thought to ask Adelaide's opinion, but decided it was best if he kept his own counsel. He had already failed Mary enough times without adding the pressure of his family's expectations to her worries.

When the time was right, he would speak to her.

Stepping out into High Street, he turned in the direction of the inn and began to walk. His morning had been a success. Apart from all the gifts, he had also bought two new bottles of black writing ink and some extra parchment. He had even remembered to get the small silk bags that Ewan had requested for giving coins to the castle staff on Handsel Monday.

He was quietly pleased with himself; for once he was organized for Christmas. He did, however, make a mental note to write out a long list once he got back to the inn—just in case he had stayed true to form and forgotten something of importance.

Crossing over High Street, he spied McNally's sweet shop. His stomach rumbled at the thought of Scottish tablet, and he made a beeline for the front door.

"Hugh."

A sudden voice from his right stirred him from his single-minded mission. Coming toward him was Mary, a small parcel tucked under her arm. He gave her a friendly greeting. "Hello."

He nodded toward the parcel. "Anything exciting?"

She shook her head. "No. Just woolen stockings. I never realized Scotland would be this cold."

As she neared, he could see she was holding the parcel close to herself, and her shoulders were scrunched up. A wave of pity swept over him the instant he realized Mary was shivering. He ached to pull her into his arms and protect her from the wind.

If she was suffering in the relative warmth of Edinburgh, Mary was in for a miserable time in the frigid climes of Strathmore Mountain. He smiled as a thought came to him. He now had the perfect opportunity to try and make up for some of his thoughtless behavior—to show Mary that she was indeed important to him.

"Did you by chance get an opportunity to go to Butlers with Adelaide?" he asked. Butlers in Edinburgh sold all manner of clothing, from hats and scarfs, through to greatcoats and boots, and everything in between.

"No. We passed it on the way through to some other shops and she pointed it out to me. They are by royal appointment to the king, are they not?" she replied.

"And the Duke of Strathmore," he said.

The look of delighted surprise on her face made his heart beat a little faster.

Hugh offered Mary his arm. "Come. You cannot visit Edinburgh without setting foot inside Butlers, especially when you are a guest of one of its patrons."

She took his arm and his heart soared. They had walked together through the university grounds over the years, but never once had he dared dream that he would be walking arm in arm with her in the middle of Edinburgh.

With her hand on his arm, he knew she was where she was meant to be. He nodded his greetings to other people as they headed back up the Royal Mile, all the while indulging in a pleasant fantasy that they were a married couple, and this was something they did every day.

The short walk to Butlers soon had Hugh's mind racing with other ideas. He would buy Mary a pair of sensible wool-lined leather gloves. Yes, that would do. No. A thick scarf and gloves was what she needed. And a coat.

By the time the doorman at Butlers ushered them inside, Hugh had a plan firmly set in his mind. Mary would not feel the cold for one moment if he had anything to say about it.

As a nearby shop assistant made his way toward them, Hugh straightened his shoulders and turned to Mary.

"I am so sorry," he said.

She scowled. "What for?"

"For being an ass. I forgot your Christmas present in Cambridge because I was too caught up in my concerns. And I wasn't there for you when you were asked to leave the university. It was selfish of me. So, I am begging your indulgence to allow me to make a small step toward the restitution of our friendship," he said.

"Oh, Hugh," she murmured.

The shop assistant stopped in front of them and bowed low. "Welcome to Butlers. How may I be of assistance to you today?"

Hugh turned and smiled at the man. "Good morning, I am Lord Hugh Radley, and this is my friend Miss Mary Gray. Miss Gray is staying with my family at Strathmore Castle for Christmas. As her wardrobe is more suited to the warmer climes of England, I was thinking she might need kitting out with a full Scottish wardrobe. What do you think?"

Mary's mouth opened, but Hugh ignored her attempted protest.

The shop assistant held his hands together tightly; a nice Christmas commission would come from such a sale. "I could not agree more, my lord. May I suggest we begin with a pair of tackety half-boots to ensure Miss Gray has a sure footing in the snow, and then move on to the woolens section?"

"Perfect."

Mary's cheeks continued to burn until they finally left Butlers several hours later. In that time, Hugh had spent, in her opinion, an outrageous sum of money on a new wardrobe for her. Her second attempt at protesting over his extravagance was ignored by both Hugh and the shop assistant; they were too busy deciding on the color of the hat which was to go with her new coat.

But it was not just the amount of money Hugh had spent on her which had Mary's heart racing. It was the brief and often light touches of his hand whenever he drew near. When he handed her a pair of kid leather gloves, she felt the heat of his fingers as they brushed against hers. She trembled at his touch.

When he reached out and tucked a wayward curl behind her ear after she had finished trying on a hat, Mary didn't know where to look. A pair of piercing blue eyes met her gaze. The smile which accompanied them took her breath away.

"Since you cannot choose between the forest green one and the chocolate brown one, I think we should take both," he said. He was so close to her that she caught the hint of musk and jasmine. Hugh was wearing the cologne she had given to him.

She pretended not to look at the price tag of the hat, having already been gently scolded for wincing when she looked at the price of the coat Hugh had chosen for her earlier. He was determined to spoil her, and she knew nothing that she said would have the slightest effect on him completing his mission.

When they returned to the inn later that afternoon, Mary's faint hopes of hearing Adelaide censure her brother over his prodigality were immediately dashed.

"Oh my, aren't you the kick!" exclaimed Adelaide, her gaze moving up from Mary's green coat to her matching hat.

Mary was tempted to pinch Hugh when she saw the sly smile which sat on his lips. He seemed so very pleased with himself. Happiness made him even more handsome.

"It took the combined efforts of myself and an enthusiastic shop assistant at Butlers to win the day, but I think we all did well. Including Mary," he said.

"Yes, you did, and Mary, you look wonderful. I must confess I was going to go through the tall cupboards at the castle and see what spare winter clothes we had so that you would not freeze. It is hard to eat supper when your teeth are continually chattering," said Adelaide.

Charles appeared in the room, carrying a smiling Will. Adelaide hurriedly scooped her son up into her arms. "Did your papa rescue you from a long sleep?" she cooed.

"Actually, we both had a very long sleep. I put him down and went to have a five-minute *sieste* on the bed; the next thing I knew, it was three hours later," replied Charles.

Charles looked at Mary and her new attire, then looked back to his wife. Mary caught the slight raise of an eyebrow as he and Adelaide exchanged a knowing look.

"Well, that is good. It means you will be able to get up to him in the middle of the night and I might get some sleep," replied Adelaide.

Hugh cleared his throat. "Speaking of sleep, I thought we might like to have an early supper this evening so we can be on the road at first light. I have reserved a private dining room."

If his efforts at shopping earlier in the day had been a surprise, the fact that Hugh had made arrangements of any sort was a revelation to Mary. He was forever forgetting to eat, so much so that she suspected the toast she regularly made for him in the evenings was the only meal he ate some days.

The Hugh Radley who now stood beside her was revealing himself to be a different man to the one she had thought she knew over the last two or so years. There was something in his manner that she couldn't quite put her finger on. It intrigued her.

She had developed a habit of chancing a look in his direction every so often, continuing her ongoing private study of him. But over the past few days, there had been several occasions when she had turned to Hugh, intent on sneaking a glance, only to find him looking at her.

Just as he was doing this very moment.

She forced herself to look away, fearful that if she continued to hold his gaze that he may finally see what she was certain was written all over her face.

She was hopelessly and irretrievably in love with him.

Chapter Eight

Mary had lived a sheltered life. Her knowledge of the world, and even England for that matter, came mostly from books. With her father devoting his time to the university, there had been little opportunity for them to travel outside Cambridge. She had been to London once, but that had been for a series of lectures given by her father, and apart from a short visit to Westminster Abbey, she had seen nothing of the great city.

The trip to Scotland was proving an eye-opening experience. Edinburgh, with its cobbled streets and imposing castle, had captured her imagination. She made a promise to herself that if she was able to make her work as a tutor a success, she would set aside a little money each week so that at least once a year she could afford to travel outside of Cambridge. She longed to see more of the world.

She looked around the travel coach. Adelaide and Charles were busy with William. Charles softly singing a French lullaby to his son, while his wife held Will in her arms and stared lovingly at her husband. Mary felt her heart swell as she watched the devoted couple and their baby. From the happy gurgles of Will, it was obvious he enjoyed hearing his father's dulcet tones.

Hugh sat beside Mary on the bench. For once he did not have his nose in a book. He was staring out the window, the hint of a smile on his face.

The coach had turned off the main road not far from Falkirk several hours earlier, and as they made their way along the narrow side road which led to Strathmore Mountain, Mary could see the landscape changing. The wooded Lowlands gave way to sweeping snow-covered meadows framed by towering mountains. The peaks of the mountains were hidden from view by low gray clouds.

Adelaide handed Will to his father and both she and Hugh pressed their faces to the window of the coach. At one point, they exchanged an excited giggle. Mary sat bemused at the sight, while Charles simply smiled.

"Walls!" cried Adelaide.

Hugh snorted. "No! Where?"

His sister held her finger to the glass. "Between the tallest of those trees. There it is again. I win."

Adelaide sat back in her seat and grinned at Hugh. "When will you ever learn? I know the exact point on the road."

A less-than-impressed-looking Hugh shook his head. "Alright, you win. *Again.*"

He turned his gaze from his sister and looked blankly at Mary. He blinked, and the vague expression on his face changed. He had registered her presence.

"Come, look," he said.

He got up and after Mary had shuffled along the bench and taken a position at the window, Hugh sat down on the other side of her. He pointed to two tall trees which stood in the middle of a nearby wood.

"There. Can you see the gray walls? Keep watching; it will come into full view any moment now," he said.

Mary peered out and she caught sight of a solid patch of gray between the trees. As the coach turned, the wood was left behind. She then got a clear view of what Adelaide and Hugh had been searching for.

Across the distance of a mile or so, beyond a small village loomed a towering Norman era stronghold. Strathmore Castle, home of the Duke of Strathmore and the Radley family.

Her mouth dropped open.

Hugh chuckled, and Adelaide clapped her hands. "Over five hundred years, never been taken," they chorused.

She had seen pictures of castles in books, and there were several real ones in the area around Cambridge, but none of them were anything like what Mary now saw. There were no ornate towers or flying buttresses. This was a stone behemoth built to withstand attack from bloodthirsty invaders.

"That is Strathmore village. Most of the castle servants live in the village and walk up the hill each morning to come to work," explained Hugh, pointing to the small collection of buildings in front of the castle.

Mighty though the imposing structure was, Mary's gaze was now drawn to the mountain beyond the castle. It dominated all that lay before it. Strathmore Mountain rose high into the sky. Its snow-capped shoulders were visible, but its peak was shrouded in thick, menacing cloud.

Mary shivered, imagining how bitterly cold it would be up on the mountain. She looked back at Hugh. "I now understand why you were so insistent on buying me that fur-lined hat."

Hugh's generous gift of winter clothing would be put to good use during her stay at Strathmore Castle.

After passing through the village, where the coach slowed down to make way for the local inhabitants on foot, and where Hugh waved out the window to everyone, they crossed over the castle's heavy wooden drawbridge and through the gateway.

Adelaide fussed with her hair as the coach entered the courtyard and drew to a halt in front of the main steps of the keep. "How do I look?"

Her husband leaned over and placed a kiss on her cheek. "*Enchanteur comme toujours*," he murmured.

Mary felt close to tears. Charles thought his wife enchanting. With such sweet endearments, it was little wonder that a minor nobleman from France had managed to capture the heart of a duke's daughter.

The door of the coach was opened by a heavily set gentleman with a long white and gray beard, who poked his head inside. Mary sat back in alarm; he must have been close to seven feet tall. A giant of a man.

"Wylcome. Well then, who would we be a havin' here?" he asked.

Hugh leaned forward. "A son and daughter of the house. Family and friend."

The gentleman looked around the carriage and stood for a moment, scratching his beard. "Hmm. I canna sae I know you. The only other son of the house was lost long ago," he replied.

Mary cast her gaze from the gentleman to Hugh and back again. She suspected there was some sort of byplay happening, but everyone was keeping a straight face.

Hugh broke first. "One Christmas. I missed one Christmas—am I never to be forgiven?"

He launched himself out of the carriage and into the embrace of the huge man, who wrapped him in a bear hug.

"Lord Hugh? Why, I didn't recognize ya. The prodigal son has returned!" he cried.

Charles climbed out next and then helped Adelaide down. She held Will in her arms. At the sight of her, the man-mountain set Hugh aside and bowed low.

"Wylcome home, Lady Adelaide," he said.

Adelaide immediately handed her firstborn over to him. As Will's eyes settled on the hulking stranger who held him, Mary gripped the door of the carriage. Any moment now she expected the infant to be registering his protest. Instead, he softly gurgled and wrapped his hand as best as he could around one of the man's thick fingers.

"So, this is William. He is a fine bairn. He is as hairy as a wild mountain boar!"

Mary laughed, but her mirth quickly died when the man mountain caught her eye. With Will still safely held in the crook of his arm, he reached out a hand to her. A blushing Mary took it and stepped down into the castle courtyard.

A murmur rippled through the other castle servants who had gathered over the past minute or so. Mary caught a whispered, "Who is that?"

It only took a sideways glance from him in the direction of the gathered servants, and they all fell silent.

"Wylcome to Strathmore Castle," he said.

Hugh hurried to Mary's side. "Master Crowdie, may I present my guest, Miss Mary Gray of Cambridge."

Having never met many lords or ladies, Mary was not completely au fait with the rules of noble society, but she knew enough to understand that if Hugh was addressing Master Crowdie in such a manner, then he must be an important man.

"Mary, Master Crowdie is the steward of Strathmore Castle. Nothing happens within the walls of the castle and the village without his say so," explained Hugh.

"Really? And here was I thinking I was in charge." A tall fair-haired man stepped up to Hugh and slapped him hard on the back.

Hugh embraced the interloper. "Brother."

Ewan Radley, Duke of Strathmore, was dressed exactly how Mary had imagined a Scottish lord would be, right down to the tartan kilt and thick black coat. She recognized the black, gray, and blue of the Strathmore plaid from the scarf which Hugh regularly wore.

"And you brought a surprise for me—excellent," said Ewan.

Mary dipped into her best curtsey as the duke caught her gaze. Her left knee wavered as she rose, and Ewan stepped forward to stop her from toppling over. He held her gaze as well as her arm, and she immediately noticed the similarity between him and Hugh. There was no mistaking that they were brothers.

"Your grace," she said.

"So, you are Miss Gray. I have heard a lot about you over the past few years. May I offer my condolences on the passing of your father."

She accepted his kind words with a smile. "Thank you."

Ewan then looked to Adelaide. "Unless you have a duke and duchess hidden in your luggage, I take it that Anne and Mowbray will not be joining us for Christmas?"

Adelaide shook her head. "Don't get me started on the pair of them. With their constant rows, I am glad that Mowbray threw a tantrum and refused to come. I am certain I would have murdered the pair of them within an hour of us leaving London if they had graced us with their company."

Hugh offered Mary his arm and the travel party followed Ewan over to the steps of the keep. Assembled on the steps was a trio of women. All three wore Strathmore tartan sashes over blue woolen gowns.

The youngest of the women, who Mary guessed was Caroline, the Duchess of Strathmore, was holding a wriggling toddler in her arms. As the arrivals approached, she handed the child over to a nursemaid and headed down the stairs. She greeted her family members with hugs and kisses before fussing over baby Will who had been safely retrieved by his father.

"It is so good to see you all. I hope the journey north wasn't too taxing on you," she said. Her eyes were fixed on Will as she spoke the words.

"He slept most of the way, for which I am eternally grateful," replied Adelaide.

"Wait until he is a toddler. David has almost inexhaustible energy," replied Caroline.

When Caroline turned to Hugh, he stepped forward with Mary. At that moment, the other women made their way down to them.

"Your graces, Lady Maude, may I present Miss Mary Gray of Cambridge. Mary is joining us for Christmas and Hogmanay," he said.

The matching smiles which appeared on their faces had Mary suddenly feeling like she was the cream and they were a pounce of cats.

"Mary. A pleasure to meet you. I am Caroline, Duchess of Strathmore. This is Lady Alison, the Dowager Duchess of Strathmore, and Lady Maude, her sister-in-law."

Mary looked down at Caroline's offered hand. She had never met a duchess before, let alone two. She dipped into another deep curtsey, holding tightly onto Hugh's hand, and prayed that her legs would not fail her this time.

"Hugh, you made it," said Lady Alison.

Hugh placed a dutiful kiss on his mother's cheek. "Mama."

She snorted. "A whole year away from home and all I get is a peck on the cheek. Unhand your lady friend and give your mother a proper greeting."

Mary caught the blush on Hugh's cheeks as he released her hand and embraced his mother. Lady Maude then stepped up for her hug, followed by Caroline. If he had thought he was going to make an understated return home, the womenfolk of the castle clearly had other ideas.

Her own soft chortle ended as soon as she saw Lady Alison's arms held out in greeting to her. "Come now. If you are a friend of my son, you shall also be greeted properly."

With no choice but to accept the welcome hugs from Hugh's female relatives, Mary submitted. Lady Alison's embrace was a little longer than the others, and the smile which sat on the dowager duchess's face when they finally parted was enough to give Mary pause.

Her unwed son had brought a young woman home for Christmas, and Lady Alison had drawn an obvious conclusion.

As Mary took Hugh's offered arm once more, and they followed the rest of the Radley family into the castle keep, Mary pondered the prudency of having come to Strathmore Castle. Hugh might be blind to her love for him, but having now met his mother, she doubted that Lady Alison was cursed with the same affliction.

As Lady Alison glanced back over her shoulder at her son and then to her, Mary wondered how long it would be before the dowager duchess took her aside and began to ask probing questions. From the glint in Lady Alison's eyes, she deduced it would not be long.

Chapter Nine

✿✿✿

Mary's first encounter with having her own maid was a touch awkward. Having gone back to the coach to retrieve her travel bag, she was politely informed that all her things had been brought inside and were waiting for her in her room.

Her room within the castle, it transpired, was more of a small apartment than a simple bedroom. It had a separate sitting room as well as two bedrooms. The walls were decorated with wallpaper in the Strathmore tartan. Mary was grateful that the imposing theme did not carry to the plush blue carpet on the floor.

A maid was busy unwrapping the parcels of clothes that Hugh had bought for Mary in Edinburgh. As soon as she saw the maid untying the string which held the parcels together, Mary hurried over.

"Oh, please, let me do that. You don't need to," she said.

The maid frowned. "It's nae bother, miss; this is ma job. I won't take long. I will hang your things up in the wardrobe and then be leavin'. If you need anything else after that, either pull on the bell here or find a footman. There is always someone about the castle who can help."

Mary's hopes to unwrap the new clothes herself and spend time admiring them were scuttled by her unexpected social status of being an honored guest of the house.

Making short work of unpacking Mary's things, the maid hung everything in the oversized oak wardrobe, she then gave a quick bob of a curtsey before leaving.

With the maid finally gone, a slightly frazzled Mary sat down on the well-appointed sofa which graced her sitting room. The furnishings of the room spoke of an opulent lifestyle she could only imagine living. After pulling off her gloves, she let her fingers touch the soft black leather. With her fingertips barely skimming the surface of the sofa, she lay back and closed her eyes.

"This is bliss," she whispered to herself

A soft tap on the door roused her some time later. Blinking, and wiping sleep from her eyes, she opened it. Hugh was standing on the threshold.

"Do you have everything you need? Has your maid been in to attend to your garments?" he asked.

"Yes, I have everything, thank you. But I wasn't sure what I was supposed to do with the maid, do I pay her?" she replied. Her greatest fear was that she would somehow put a foot wrong and have the castle staff think her rude. Was she supposed to tip the staff like porters at a hotel? She had heard that was the proper thing to do. She would leave a coin for the maid next time just to be sure.

"Just let them go about their work; they are here to help you. You only have to ask. And no, you don't need to pay her," he said.

It was nice to have a maid, but she was not comfortable with the idea. A few weeks in Scotland would spoil her for the life she had waiting for her back in Cambridge. No one would be pressing her gowns for her once she returned to England. The furniture in her cramped bedsit would consist of a small bed and a single chair.

Hugh's gaze went to her hair, and the hint of a shy smile appeared on his face. "I was waiting in the great hall for you to make an appearance, but when you didn't, I thought I should come and find you. You look like you took the opportunity for a nap."

She put a hand to her hair. The soft chignon she had fashioned that morning had fallen, and badly needed repair. "I sat to rest my eyes and must have fallen asleep."

Hugh stopped a passing footman and murmured instructions. The footman nodded, then hurried away.

"I have asked that your maid attend to you and fix your hair. I thought you might like to take a stroll around the castle once you are ready. Make sure you dress warm."

Mary frowned. She had been managing her hair since she was a little girl; the thought of sitting while a maid attended to it struck her as odd.

Hugh leaned in and took hold of her hand. "Enjoy your time here and let the castle servants assist you. If you don't, then they will think they have done something wrong. And then we shall have Master Crowdie having a word with my brother, and eventually I will be taken aside and spoken to. So please, let your maid, whose name is Heather, fix your hair."

After Hugh made the proper introductions, he left Mary and Heather to overcome their initial awkward start. While Heather set Mary's hair, they discussed a daily routine which would suit them both. Once Mary's chignon had been set to right, she retrieved her new fur hat from the cupboard.

"Do you have any hatpins, miss?" asked Heather

"No. I forgot them." Her only good hatpin had recently broken, and she had decided replacing it could wait until she had more money.

"I shall see if I can find you some, but in the meantime, you will have tae watch out for the wind. It does loves tae steal the hat from your head," said Heather.

Heather left the room singing a happy little ditty, leaving Mary to finish dressing for her walk with Hugh. With her new thick coat buttoned to the neck, Mary was as warm as toast. She stuffed her gloves into her pockets, then stood back and looked at herself in the mirror.

She cut a fine figure in her new, expensive clothes. Perhaps now Hugh would notice her. His efforts in Edinburgh had given her the first real glimmer of hope that he did see the Mary beyond the girl who brought him coffee and toast.

The clothes were wonderful. But it was the attention Hugh had given her all that afternoon, the words of encouragement for every item she tried on, and the small affectionate touches of his hand that had set her heart racing.

"Don't be silly, and don't get your hopes up. This is Hugh," she cautioned herself.

At some point, he would break her heart and, knowing the sweet and often baffle-headed man that he was, Hugh would likely have no idea what he had done.

She met him downstairs a short time later. The great hall reminded her of the dining halls at St John's College, though the long dining tables were missing. The hall itself was divided up into several living areas, with large tapestries hanging from the roof to create the illusion of separate rooms.

Hugh nodded at the tapestries. "My father had them installed. He decided that the castle no longer needed to be a great meeting place, but rather somewhere that his family could live. We move all the furniture out of the way and replace it with tables for events such as Hogmanay," he explained.

"And Christmas?"

He shook his head. "Not in Scotland. Christmas is not celebrated widely here. The Church of Scotland doesn't hold with the holy day, so the Radley family celebrates it privately, and then hosts the big celebration over New Year's."

Hugh had never struck her as being a typical Scotsman. He didn't have much of a lilt in his voice, and only the use of the occasional Scottish word indicated that he was anything other than a full-blooded Englishman.

"Come. Let me show you the castle. The weather is still fine, but Master Crowdie tells me we will be in for a major frost overnight, and possibly snow."

Mary followed him out of the great hall, expecting to turn right and venture into the courtyard, but Hugh turned left and headed for a set of nearby stone steps.

"You will want your gloves and hat held on tight where we are going," he said.

"And where is that?"

"The ramparts."

He put one foot on the bottom stone step, then held out his hand to her. Mary took it. If she had thought he was being a little overprotective about her climbing the steps, she soon understood his reasoning.

The steps wound tightly around the staircase, hugging close to the wall. In some places the stones had been worn away so badly that she had to avoid the step and take two at a time. She was hot and huffing by the time they finally reached the top of the castle.

Hugh stopped at a huge door made from hard elm and looked back the way they had come. When he let go of her hand, Mary sensed the loss. His strong grip as he led her up the stairs had been an interesting revelation. The quiet, bookish Hugh Radley was a man of unknown physical strength.

"Ewan is going to get a stonemason over from Glasgow to look at rebuilding the steps. They may have served their purpose when this was a fortified castle, but now they just make it difficult to carry things up and down," said Hugh.

He pushed on the door and stepped through it. Mary followed him out into bright sunshine. She held her hand up to shield her eyes from the sun. At the same time, a sudden blast of chill wind tore at her hat. It flew from her head and landed on the stone rampart, where the wind quickly picked it up once more and skipped it out of reach.

"Oh!" She went to step past Hugh to rescue her hat, but he moved in front of her.

Bent low, he chased after it. His sure-footed leaps from one side of the narrow ramparts to the next showed how much at home he was on top of the castle.

With a deftly timed sweep of his hand, he finally caught Mary's hat. She applauded his success as he spun around on one foot and held it up, a triumphant smile on his face.

"Well done, Hugh."

He trotted back to her and with a flourish, returned the hat to its rightful owner. A familiar flash of heat raced down her spine as their gazes met. Mary held the tight smile she had perfected for such moments with him; she dared not reveal the full smile her heart so desperately craved to give him. *A heart not risked is a heart not broken.*

She held the hat firmly in her hand, not wanting to add its loss to the cost of replacing her hatpin.

The wind on the ramparts was fierce and unrelenting, but Hugh did not seem to mind. While Mary was busy trying to keep her hair out of her face and protect her ears from the stinging cold, he went about with only a coat and scarf to keep the elements at bay.

When they finally managed to find a spot out of the wind, it took her a good minute or so to pin her hair back. Heather's earlier efforts at fixing Mary's hairstyle had been blown away.

"If you look over there, you can see Castle Hill. On top of it is Stirling Castle. That's where a number of the kings and queens of Scotland were crowned," he said, pointing to a tall crag in the distance.

"Including Mary Queen of Scots," replied Mary. She may not have travelled much in her life, but she knew her history. Access to the extensive library was one of the privileges of having grown up at Cambridge University.

"Now that I have a better understanding of where Strathmore Castle is situated, I realize there are a number of significant historical sites around here. Bannockburn, where Robert the Bruce defeated the English, must be only a few miles away," she added.

"That's it there. It's about fifteen miles as the crow flies," Hugh replied, pointing to a flat area toward one side of another hill. "The Bruce used Strathmore Castle as a staging ground for his troops before the battle of Bannockburn, though it was not as complete a castle then as it is now."

Mary heard the fierce pride in Hugh's voice as he spoke. Every moment that she spent with him in this place showed him in a different light. And every moment, her love for him grew.

She turned away from the view over the battlements and forced herself to take several long deep breaths.

"I am glad you came. I hadn't realized how much it would mean to me to show you my home," said Hugh.

Mary nodded, incapable of speech. The next few weeks here with him at the castle were going to be a trial for her heart. The way he made her feel, she feared she may not survive it.

Chapter Ten

Hugh had initially thought to simply show Mary around the castle and introduce her to a few of the castle stalwarts—people he trusted and loved—but by the time they returned to the keep, he sensed something else was at play. From the moment he had taken her by the hand and led her up the castle steps, his perception of her had begun to change.

Several times over the past days he had caught her staring at him, an odd expression on her face, as if she was studying him. And then at other times when he looked, she seemed distant and closed off from him, as if lost in herself.

He recognized himself in that behavior, knowing that he often retreated into his own thoughts to escape from the world. *And what is it that you seek to escape from Miss Mary Gray?*

"Ah, there you are. We were speculating as to where you had got to," said Ewan.

As Hugh and Mary entered the great hall, he saw the rest of the Radley family members all gathered near one of the castle fireplaces. A fire was burning in the huge iron grate, but even at ten feet from one side of the hearth to the other, it struggled to create much warmth in the cavernous space.

"I was just showing Mary the view from the ramparts," Hugh replied. He ignored the small shared looks that he saw exchanged between Adelaide and Charles, but the look that passed between Lady Alison and Aunt Maude gave him pause.

Not you as well. Please don't meddle.

He had expected his sister and brother-in-law to try and play cupid —Adelaide was never one for subtly—but he was more concerned by his mother and aunt's apparent interest in Mary and himself.

When he looked to Ewan, he was greeted with a raised eyebrow. He sighed, relieved that at least his brother and Lady Caroline were being sensible about things. Mary was his friend, and a guest at the castle. Whatever else developed between them from her stay in Scotland, he wanted it to be fresh and unencumbered. He had not brought her all this way simply to use the time alone with her as a means to seduce her into marriage.

He pushed his tongue against the back of his teeth, but a little voice in his brain told him it would take more than that to believe the lie he had just told himself. He wanted Mary; the question was, did she want him?

"We are heading to the village to buy some tablet if the two of you would like to come," said Adelaide.

Hugh noted the use of the term "the two of you? and suspected it would not be the last time he heard it over the Christmas period.

He looked to Mary. She blinked, then put a hand to her face and wiped something away from her eye. *Was that a tear?*

His family were making more of the relationship between him and Mary than currently existed. A quiet word or two might need to be had to calm the matchmakers down. He did not need his family interfering with his plans, or making Mary feel uncomfortable.

"The road to the village is icy, so you will all require your tackety boots today," said Ewan.

Hugh could have hugged his brother for the delicate change of subject.

"Well then, it is fortunate that Hugh procured Mary a pair of boots along with a number of other items of clothing while we were in Edinburgh," said Adelaide.

Hugh could have swatted his sister for the not-so-delicate remark.

"Right then. So, if everyone who needs to change their boots can go and do so, the rest of us will wait here and then we can all walk to the village together," said Aunt Maude.

～

Hugh watched with interest as Mary made her first tentative steps in her new boots. "How do they feel on your feet?" he asked.

"A little strange when I place my feet on the road, but they are comfortable. I never thought to actually wear boots with metal plates and nails in them," replied Mary.

"That's because you have never been to Scotland and had to walk on black ice," said Aunt Maude.

The party of six, Caroline and Ewan having stayed behind at the castle, were making their way down the road to Strathmore village. The walk, if it could be described as such, was a constant game of side-stepping hazards. The road surface was covered with icy patches, interspersed with frozen puddles of muddy water. Every step held the promise of a hard and wet landing for an unsure foot.

Hugh had offered Mary his arm, but she told him she needed to learn to walk in her new boots. He accepted her reasons with good grace, but still walked close enough so that he could rescue her if she did slip.

While he had often turned to Mary for assistance while he was at Cambridge, he now found himself in possession of a growing need to protect her. With her father gone, she was all alone in the world. Every time he thought that she had nearly spent Christmas by herself in a boarding house, he grew angry with himself again. He had abandoned her.

Adelaide and Charles had taken the lead in the walking party, with Lady Alison and Aunt Maude following close behind. Hugh and Mary were left to bring up the rear. His family members marched on ahead, creating an ever-growing gap between them.

Mary slipped but managed to steady herself. "Oops, nearly," she said. Hugh reached out and took her arm. He looked down and saw the patch of black ice she was standing on.

"Here, step toward me. There are some drier spots over this way," he said.

She took a step toward him, but the black ice caught her a second time. As her feet went out from under her, Hugh steadied himself and wrapped his arms around her.

They stood in silence for a moment. A little white cloud of condensation hung between them as they both breathed heavily in the cold air.

"Thank you. I am glad you are surer of foot than me," she finally said.

Her head rose, and in that instant, Hugh was certain he had been clubbed with the hilt of a highland dirk. The green eyes which held him were mesmerizing. He blinked hard. Who was this enchantress who had stolen the body of kind, helpful Mary? His love for her had coalesced into something deeper, something more powerful.

Pure. Raw. Desire.

He brushed a hand on her cheek and leaned in close. His heart was hammering in his chest. Closer. She batted her long eyelashes. Closer. Her lips parted. *Closer.*

"Come on, you two, we need to get to Dunn's before nightfall!" bellowed Maude.

Hugh muttered several very un-Christmas-like words under his breath as Mary turned her head away. He waved to his family, who he was not surprised to see were all staring daggers at Maude.

"Coming," he replied through gritted teeth.

In the village, they headed for the local store: Dunn's. As soon as she stepped inside, Mary felt immediately at home. Unlike the fancy shops in Edinburgh, Dunn's was more like the usual places where Mary shopped in Cambridge. A one-stop shop for most things.

"Have you ever tried tablet before?" asked Hugh.

"No. What is it?" replied Mary.

"It's made from sugar and cream," said Hugh, handing her a piece.

"And a dram of whisky if you have any self-respect," added Maude.

Mary popped the tablet into her mouth. The buttery confection was a delight. So chewy and yet so soft. She hummed with happiness.

She wiped the sugary crumbs from her lips, then licked her finger. "That was marvelous," she said.

Hugh offered her another piece. Then, for some inexplicable reason, he stood and watched her eat it. When she licked her fingers again, she was certain she heard him swallow deep. The barest hint of a moan escaped his lips.

He quickly returned to the counter and purchased another two bags of tablet, handing them both to Mary who put them into the pocket of her new coat.

Before they left the village shop, Mary made a mental note of some inexpensive items which would make suitable Christmas gifts. With a little more practice in her hobnail boots, she felt confident that in time she could make the trip back to the village on her own.

"Thank you, Mister Dunn. As always, it is a pleasure to visit your shop," said Lady Alison, as they finalized their purchases and made for the door. Aunt Maude stuffed a boiled sweet into her mouth and nodded her agreement.

Mary allowed Hugh to take her arm for the return walk home. She told herself it was purely for safety's sake and to please Hugh. She was his guest and should not refuse him any kindness he wished to bestow upon her.

She pulled the bag of tablet from out of her coat pocket and offered it to him. With a polite 'thank you' and a smile which had her blinking hard, he took out two pieces. He handed the largest piece to Mary and popped the other one into his mouth.

"Thank you," she said.

"For what?"

"For the delicious tablet. For saving me on the road earlier. Just everything." As she placed her arm once more in his, Mary made a fateful decision. She would not hold back from enjoying this Christmas. Wherever she spent her next Christmas, she would always have this one to remember him by. A happy memory of a treasured friendship. Of a love that, though it was unrequited, still gave her joy.

After New Year's she would return to England, and she would let him go.

As Hugh and Mary led the way home, Lady Alison took a hold of her daughter's arm. She smiled at Adelaide.

"It is lovely to have you home, my darling. And wonderful to be able to hold my new grandson. You and I need to catch up on so much."

Adelaide raised an eyebrow. "Thank you, Mama. It is wonderful to be home in Scotland. Is there anything particularly pressing that you wish to discuss with me?"

Lady Alison leaned in close. "Well, since you asked. May I enquire as to whether you were able to secure a particular item in Edinburgh?"

Adelaide gently patted her mother's arm. "You didn't think I would dare to arrive without it, did you? Charles had it well hidden in our luggage."

Lady Alison softly chortled. "Well done, my dear. Now it just remains to see if we can make magic happen a second time."

Aunt Maude followed behind, tucking into her bag of boiled sweets before offering one to Charles who walked alongside her.

"Witchcraft at Christmas, hmm," she gruffly remarked.

Chapter Eleven

T he whisky hit the back of Mary's throat, and she held a hand
to her chest. Heat coursed through her body, right to her
toes.

"I have had a hot toddy before, but never straight whisky. I can see
why you would need a bottle or two of it here to see you through
winter," she said.

After their visit to the village, Mary had been stolen away from
Hugh and pressed into service by the women. While the great hall was
to be utilized by the family for a small Christmas gathering, its main
purpose was as a place for all the castle staff and villagers to gather for
Hogmanay at New Year's.

"It is not officially Hogmanay until you can smell the wild boar
roasting over the fire pits in the center of the castle courtyard," said
Lady Alison.

Aunt Maude rubbed her hands. "I cannae wait."

Mary was surprised to see the Radley women dressed in simple
brown woolen gowns with aprons. The dowager duchess held a
broom in her hand, and she was sweeping ash from around the
fireplace.

Maude was seated in a chair, tying together bundles of what

appeared to be small branches of juniper. Beside her on the floor sat an impressive pile of completed work.

"Hogmanay traditions are to be kept. The first one is for the women of the family to clean the castle from top to bottom. It's like spring cleaning in England, only the redding is done in preparation for New Year's Day," explained Lady Alison.

"Redding?" replied Mary.

"We clean the house now, then at Hogmanay we sweep all the ash from the fireplace so that our home is clean for the start of the new year. We light the juniper bundles and walk them around the castle to ward off bad spirits from the old year. The other bundles are for the villagers to take with them and perform the ceremony in their homes."

Lady Alison handed Mary the broom and pointed to the back of the great hall. Mary was used to cleaning the small apartment at the university, so domestic work was not an issue. What did have her gripping the broom handle tight was the notion that she was considered a member of the family.

"If you would like to start sweeping from the back, I will get another broom and work in from the sides. Oh, and don't fret over the rest of the castle; it was all done last week. I wouldn't press you into service in such a way on your first Christmas here," she said.

First Christmas.

Mary caught the remark. It sounded like Lady Alison expected to see her at Strathmore Castle in future years; not just this one. If only that could be.

Adelaide and Lady Caroline appeared at the foot of the stairs. Adelaide carried a red box in her hands, holding it with obvious reverence as she walked into the great hall. Mary could only imagine what precious treasure was contained within.

Adelaide set the box down on a table out of the way of where the women were working. "Nearly time," she said.

Lady Caroline took a seat in a nearby chair while Adelaide picked up a dust cloth and began to bustle about the great hall, dusting and polishing every surface as she went. Lady Alison came and spoke to Lady Caroline, who said only a few words before rising from her chair and leaving the room.

As she passed, Mary could see that she was pale, and her features drawn. She gave Mary a wan smile as she made her way to the stairs. The duchess had been quiet the whole time, barely saying anything beyond the minimum required by good manners.

Two castle servants appeared at the front door of the great hall. One carried a wooden step and hammer, while his companion had a large coil of rope hanging over his shoulder and a piece of wood in his hand.

They bowed to Lady Alison, and she pointed toward a spot on the floor. "That should do nicely. If I recall, that is the same spot we used last year."

The man with the rope took the piece of wood and tied them together. He then stood on the stool and began to throw the wood up toward one of the oak beams which supported the roof of the great hall. His colleague held onto the other end of the rope.

Mary stopped her sweeping and, along with the others, watched in silent fascination at the goings on. On the fourth attempt, the wood cleared the beam and then came rattling back toward the floor. The servant holding the rope pulled back, stopping the wood before it could hit the ground. He tied off a knot in the rope, but left the wood hanging.

With this piece of work now complete, the two men stood back from the stool.

Adelaide put down her dust cloth and retrieved the box she had brought with her. With a curtsy to her mother, she handed it over.

"Lady Caroline is indisposed this afternoon and has asked that I continue my role for this year," announced Lady Alison.

Mary set her broom aside and walked over to where the others stood. She was eager to see what item of importance lay within the box that warranted such a ceremony.

Lady Alison removed the black ribbons which held the box closed and handed them to Adelaide. With great reverence, the lid was lifted. Mary and Aunt Maude both leaned in close, peaking over the side of the box.

A golden ball of mistletoe sat before them.

Aunt Maude and Lady Alison both gasped. The castle servants turned and bowed low to Adelaide.

Mary didn't know where to look. All this had been for a branch of mistletoe. She stifled a nervous laugh.

"Absolutely magnificent. Adelaide, you have done your family proud," whispered Lady Alison. A soft smile sat on Aunt Maude's face.

Mary's clear lack of understanding of the significance of the moment, together with her embarrassment, were saved by the arrival of Ewan, Hugh, and Charles through the front doors of the great hall.

With a solemn look on his face, the Duke of Strathmore strode over to where the mistletoe lay in the box. He looked down, paused for a moment, then nodded. "Near-perfect formation. Bright coloring. And just the right amount of branch on the end. I couldn't have chosen better myself."

"I know," replied Adelaide.

Ewan chuckled at his sister's words. "Now to get this beast up where it belongs."

After the hammer and a nail were handed to him, Ewan set to work attaching the branch of the mistletoe to the piece of wood. Several more nails were added before he stood back and declared that the job was done.

Everyone watched while the wood was hauled back into the air, coming to rest some ten feet above the floor. The rope was then tied off a second time with a firm knot.

Hugh came to Mary's side. "The hanging of the mistletoe is a very important part of the annual festivities. I am glad you were here to be able to witness it," he said.

She felt safe enough to ask him the obvious question. "I know people in England see it as a fun part of Christmas—most everyone has kissed under the mistletoe — but why is it so important here?"

"Because it holds real magic," he whispered.

She met his eyes. Hugh was about to become a curate for the Church of England, and yet here he was talking about magic. She had never known him to be anything other than serious about matters of his faith and life's calling.

"It's alright; I won't get thrown out of the church for respecting old customs and ways. All forms of religion have a degree of believing in something we don't fully understand," he said.

If her father could hear Hugh right now, he would be frowning with disapproval. Professor James Gray had been strict to the letter in his observance of the scriptures.

"This is Scotland; we do things a little differently here," he added.

With the mistletoe now in place, eager looks passed between the members of the gathering.

Charles slipped an arm around Adelaide's waist and drew her to him. She pretended to bat away his amorous advances but did not put up a fight when her husband steered her in the direction of the mistletoe.

"Just remember that with great power comes great responsibility. We expect to hear word of a new arrival from the two of you if you dare to kiss under the Strathmore mistletoe," said Ewan.

Charles laughed, and taking his wife in his arms, he gave her a soft, loving kiss.

Applause rippled throughout the great hall. The mistletoe had captured its first couple.

"And there will be many more before it comes down after Hogmanay. I wonder who will be next," said Adelaide.

Mary kept her gaze fixed on the rest of the group, quietly praying that Hugh did not see the heat which she felt burning on her cheeks. She could only pray that she was one of those whom the magic of the mistletoe would touch.

Chapter Twelve

✦✦✦

Hugh hadn't failed to see the bright red of Mary's cheeks as she watched Charles and Adelaide embrace.

No one who witnessed the kiss could have been left unaffected. French-born Charles Alexandre wore his passion for his wife on his sleeve. Hugh sensed a small pang of jealousy toward his sister and her joyful union, but he chided himself for it. Adelaide had found Charles after a long period of heartbreak and deserved every moment of happiness.

After the mistletoe ceremony, Mary slipped from the great hall. Hugh spent the rest of the afternoon in Ewan's study, discussing estate matters. He was not the duke, but as the second son of the house, and heir presumptive, he still had his duties to perform.

"Now I have tallied up the heads to receive Handsel Monday coin purses, and it stands at fifty-seven. Master Crowdie has confirmed the number," said Ewan.

Hugh sat and stared at his hands; his mind was completely elsewhere. His thoughts focused solely on Mary.

"I thought we should give every man one hundred pounds."

One hundred pounds.

"What?!" replied Hugh.

Ewan sat and stared at his brother. "I thought that might get your attention. I know you find estate matters a tad boring, but if you could just concentrate for a few minutes, then you can go back into the hall and continue to make doe eyes at Miss Mary Gray."

Hugh had been caught daydreaming, a fact he could not deny. "Is it that obvious?"

Ewan chuckled. "Yes. Do you remember when I had a small thing for Lord Stirling's daughter some years ago? Well, the look I wore on my face all that summer is the very same one you have had plastered to your face since you got here. I'm surprised that the two of you are not already betrothed."

"Her father was my professor, and so pursuing his daughter would not have been proper. And now that she is alone, it is going to be difficult to convince her that I am acting beyond mere pity for her changed circumstances. Add to that the fact that I do not know if she holds any romantic feelings for me, and you will have an understanding of how complicated this situation actually is," replied Hugh.

Ewan sat back in his chair with a look of serious contemplation on his face. If anyone had an appreciation of dealing with a complicated love life, it was him. He had thrown Lady Caroline Hastings over in order to marry her sister, only to be jilted by his fiancée who had died while giving birth to his illegitimate son. It was a miracle he had managed to win Caroline back and secure her hand in marriage.

"The only advice I can give you, if you are asking for it, is to be honest with her. It took some time for me to come to that realization when Caroline and I were estranged. Make a promise to yourself that before New Year's, you will talk to Mary and tell her how you feel. It was the only thing that brought Caroline back to me in the end."

"Yes."

"Oh, and don't let Mama or any of the others try to play cupid. They got away with it, last Christmas, but that is because they had my infant son David to wave under Caroline's nose. You don't have the luxury of a sweet-faced bairn to win Mary over to you."

"Try just a bite."

Mary looked at the ladle and screwed up her face. Hugh tried not to laugh. It had taken more than a little coaxing to get her to consider attempting a mouthful of haggis. But now that it sat before her on the spoon, she hesitated.

"Couldn't I have another piece of the blackbun instead?" she said.

"No. The rest of the blackbun is for Hogmanay. We only got to try some today because cook had made an extra batch. Come on, you have to try a spot of haggis; it is the law." He waved the ladle under her nose, laughing when she finally opened her mouth and let him feed her. She didn't chew for a moment, a look of distaste evident on her face. Offal was not to everyone's liking.

Then, to his delight, her face changed.

As she chewed, her eyes grew wide. She swallowed. "That was not at all what I expected. It was nutty and peppery."

"Cook adds a lot of spices to it. Once you get over the idea that it is the heart, liver, and lungs of the sheep, it's quite a good meat," he replied.

He offered her a second spoonful and grinned when she accepted it without hesitation. For someone who had lived a sheltered life at the university, he was pleased to see that Mary was open to embracing new experiences.

The family were gathered in the great hall for supper. The great space had been cleaned from top to bottom. A roaring fire burned in the giant stone fireplace.

The room was a sea of Strathmore family tartan. One-year-old David was decked out in a kilt which had once been his father's, while baby Will was wrapped up warmly in a tartan shawl. Everyone wore the family plaid. Everyone except Mary.

Hugh had broached the subject of giving Mary a Strathmore tartan stole to wear, but Ewan had refused. Only family could wear it. Hugh understood his brother's message loud and clear. If he wanted Mary to wear the tartan, he had to make her one of the family.

Lady Caroline finally made an appearance in the great hall just before supper. She looked brighter than she had been earlier in the day but was still pale. As she came to her husband's side, Ewan drew her in close and spoke to her. She smiled and nodded.

"Could I please have your attention for a moment," announced Ewan.

He bent down and lifted David into his arms. Lady Caroline stood close.

"This time last year, I was fortunate to make Caroline my wife. In doing so, David gained a mother, and the castle its new duchess. Today, I am happy to announce that Caroline and I are to have our first child together in the new year."

Ewan's words had the immediate effect of Adelaide squealing with delight, Lady Alison giving a knowing nod of the head, and Aunt Maude searching her pockets for a handkerchief. Mary stood with her hands clasped together, held to her lips.

Before anyone had the chance to step forward and congratulate the expectant mother, her husband gently steered her to the place under the mistletoe. Charles took David from his father.

"You have made this first year of our marriage the happiest year of my life. Thank you for making me your husband." Ewan placed his hands on Caroline's cheeks and bent his head. Caroline wrapped her arms around his waist and gave herself up to the kiss.

Hugh discovered there was something in his eye and quickly wiped it away, noting that he was not the only one who had experienced a sudden eye irritation.

"Oh," Mary softly sighed.

He tore his gaze from the amorous couple and looked at her. The longing he saw in her eyes had him swallowing the lump which had formed in his throat. She too wiped away tears.

"You have such a loving family," she said, turning to him.

Hugh studied her face for a moment. How many times had he seen that same look on Mary's countenance as she brought him toast and coffee? It was there every time she had encouraged him to study a little later, to make his university paper better.

And until this moment, he had not understood it. A bolt of sudden awareness hit him.

He was not alone in wishing for love.

He stayed close to Mary for the rest of the evening, ensuring she was included in all the family celebrations. He forced himself to maintain the faint smile on his face, with the result that by the time he retired for the night his cheeks hurt.

Once back in his room, the smile swiftly disappeared. He sent his valet away, unable to maintain his polite manner for a single minute longer.

The past few days had been a slow and uncomfortable revelation of how poorly he had treated Mary. While all the time she had looked at him with love and longing in her eyes, he had been more concerned with his studies and his career. He had kept her at arm's length.

She deserved better than the mere thanks he had given her every time she had shown him kindness. And she should have received far more from him than the occasional "sorry" after her father's death. Little wonder she had kept such an important issue as the loss of her home from him when he had shown so little regard for her feelings. He had made a mockery of the word *love*.

He looked down at his kilt, running his fingers along the lines of the tartan. The blue and black had been proudly taken back up by the family as soon as the ban on wearing tartan had been lifted. His hand dropped to his side; he was unworthy to wear the plaid.

Mary had a whole new winter wardrobe thanks to his need to assuage his guilt, but it was not enough. She should be wearing the Strathmore family tartan.

"I'll be damned if you are not wearing the plaid come Hogmanay night."

Now he just had to figure out a way to get Mary to understand that she held his heart, and that from now on, she would always come first.

Chapter Thirteen

Mary wondered if she could ever be comfortable in the freezing Scottish winter.

As soon as she and Hugh left the protection of the high castle walls the following morning and headed onto the lower slopes of Strathmore Mountain, the wind attacked them. Its cruel fingers pinched her face and bit through to her bones.

The chilly weather, however, was only one of her problems. The other was the odd mood which she discovered Hugh was in the moment she met him downstairs at breakfast that morning. His greeting for her was a terse "Good morning, Mary."

He'd barely acknowledged the rest of the family seated around the breakfast table, reserving his responses to their questions of him to one or two words at best.

Something was seriously amiss. She knew enough of him to know that he usually only became this taciturn during exams, and that was due to lack of sleep. But he was here, at home with his family, and he should be happy, not lost in a dark mood. She had only accepted his offer to take a stroll on the side of Strathmore Mountain so she could be alone with him and try to get to the bottom of what troubled him. She hoped he would confide in her.

"It's a brisk morning," she said, trying to lighten the mood but failing.

He nodded and gave her a curt, "Yes."

She followed him as he walked the narrow track which meandered along the side of the mountain. At one point, it broke into two sections. One track looked like it eventually became a bigger road which continued on and then disappeared to one side of the mountain. The other led up onto Strathmore Mountain.

When Hugh made to continue along the path which crossed the mountain, Mary stopped. If he wanted to share his foul mood with her, then she would rather it be somewhere warm.

He took a few more steps before he turned and look back at her. "Are you coming?"

"No. Not if you are going to be a misery guts for the duration of our walk. If I am going to freeze to death, I would prefer it was with a smile on my face. I don't know what is bothering you this morning, Hugh. If you don't tell me what is wrong, then I shall return to the castle, and you can keep your own company." Mary stood her ground. She knew her words were harsh, but her experience of Hugh was that sometimes he only responded to a gruff approach.

She nodded with some relief when his stiff shoulders slouched. Her words had reached him.

He walked back to her. "I'm sorry. I lay awake all night trying to resolve a problem. I'm still not sure if I have found the right solution."

"Try me. You know I am always someone you can turn to for advice," she replied.

A brittle hint of his usual self appeared on his face. "Yes, you are. That is another of your many wonderful traits, Mary. Though I am not so certain that you are the right person in whom I should confide, seeing as the problem concerns you."

She should have seen it coming. Hugh had held off on doing anything about the issue of the university and her living arrangements. But now, it appeared after speaking with his brother, he had come to the conclusion that there was little, if anything, he could do about it.

"You don't need to go into battle for me with the head of St John's

College. You have your new appointment at St Martin-in-the-Fields to worry about. Just let things stay as they are," she replied.

He huffed in clear annoyance at her reply. "That matter is not yet settled, but it is not what vexes me this morning."

She waited. If there was one thing, she had in abundance from dealing with students all her life, it was patience. Bitterly cold, evil wind and all, she could stand on the side of a mountain and wait him out.

His gaze drifted from her to a nearby barn. He pointed toward it. "Let's at least get out of the wind so we can talk."

When the barn door closed behind them, Mary put a hand to her ears. Her winter bonnet had kept most of her head warm, but her poor ears were stinging. "Remind me to never complain about an English winter ever again. How do you people survive?"

"Actually, it is barely winter yet. Come January, the mountain will be lost under a thick layer of snow, and even the road into the village will become impassable at times," Hugh replied.

Mary found herself a nice pile of warm, dry straw on which to sit and plopped down on it. Hugh remained standing. After pulling off one of his gloves, he rubbed it over his face.

A chill of worry settled in her stomach. It was unusual to see Hugh in such a troubled state.

She patted the straw next to her. "Come and sit down. Tell me your troubles."

With an uncertain huff, he wandered over and dropped down beside her. "Alright. Here goes nothing."

He fell silent for a time. As the seconds stretched into minutes, Mary began to wonder if he had changed his mind about confiding in her. He startled her when he finally spoke again.

"You and I are friends, are we not?" he ventured.

"Yes. I hope so," she replied.

He was laying the ground for whatever difficult conversation lay ahead. Mary picked up a piece of straw and began to nervously wrap it around her finger.

"Well, I don't want us to be friends. I mean, not just friends."

"What do you mean?"

He moved to face her, taking her hand in his. "I want you to consider becoming my wife."

Under most any other circumstance she would have rejoiced at his words, but only disappointment stirred within. Hugh had obviously thought long and hard about her perilous situation and decided that the obvious solution was to offer her marriage.

In his world, it no doubt made perfect sense. They were already friends, and with his family's wealth at his disposal, he could offer her a life of security and comfort. Problem solved.

She would be mad not to seriously consider the offer, yet her heart demanded more.

"I see," she replied.

If she married Hugh, she would have a home, and likely a family in the years to come. She would no longer be alone in the world.

But she would be alone in her love for him.

"Will you at least consider it?" he said.

She shivered, the barn no longer holding the warmth it once had. Hugh's marriage proposal, if it could be considered as one, was as cold as the chill winds on the mountain.

She tried to console herself with the knowledge that many other people had practical marriages based purely on friendship. Many of those unions seemed to work.

The challenge she now faced would be deciding if she could spend the rest of her life with him knowing he would never feel anything more than a warm regard for her. Her love for him would remain unrequited.

"I may need some time," she replied. Mary got to her feet. A dull ache of sadness sat heavy in her heart. "You have never once shown me any indication of affection, so I am going to have to assume that your reasons for offering me marriage are purely practical ones. If so then mores the pity, because my father always said that a marriage created without any heat or passion to sustain it, would eventually falter when faced with the madness that life throws at us all," she said.

She headed for the door, leaving Hugh to sit on the straw and ponder her words. She could only pray that he had it in his heart to offer her more.

"I shall see you at supper," she said.

She slipped through the barn door and headed back to the castle.

Chapter Fourteen

A s Mary disappeared, Hugh uttered a number of words that would get him thrown out of Sunday mass if anyone was to overhear them.

Mary, of course, was right. He had put as much emotion into his marriage proposal as he did when asking her for a cup of coffee. He should be counting his blessings that she had not given him a straight out *no* to his pathetic offer.

If his feeble attempt had been a university paper, he knew he would be pulling an all-night study session and resubmitting it in the morning. He could just imagine what the professor would have written on the front page in large black ink.

"D minus, lacking in effort. See me after class," he muttered.

His brother's words now came back to haunt him.

He should have been honest with her and confessed his love. If she didn't feel the same for him, then he would at least finally know the truth of where their relationship stood. But what if she did care for him? By not being brave and offering his heart, he risked never getting the chance to hear her tell him she loved him.

She couldn't be held to blame for choosing to protect her heart if she decided Hugh did not hold it in high enough regard. Love was precious.

He got to his feet. Mary hadn't said no, which was at least some small comfort. She had, however, made it clear that if he thought to marry her for the sake of convenience, he may not like her answer.

Opening the barn door, he stepped out into the fierce wind. He looked at the path which led up onto the mountain and nodded. If there was one thing the wild Scottish winter was good for, it was blowing some sense into a clouded mind. He pulled up the collar of his coat and headed up the track.

Chapter Fifteen

Hugh felt like he was treading on eggshells. Mary was polite, but cool whenever he tried to talk to her. It was a side of her he had not seen before, and if he was honest, it scared him just a little, yet it was also oddly encouraging.

If the rest of the family had noticed any difficulty between him and Mary, they were keeping it to themselves.

Toasting forks sat around the fireplace, along with a huge pot of tea. These were the nights Hugh treasured the most. Hogmanay, with its huge bonfires, whisky, and roasted wild boar was a wonderful experience, but nothing compared to the quiet evenings spent with his family in the lead up to the end-of-year celebrations.

I should have made the effort to come home last Christmas. I won't make that mistake again. And next year, I shall bring my wife with me.

Mary sat close by, nursing David on her lap. He was a bubbly little boy, full of life. He had a vocabulary of a good dozen words now, and each day he added new ones. Every time he looked at Caroline, he would point to her stomach and say "baby."

Hugh finished his first cup of tea, then stood and went to get another.

Ewan met him by the fireside. "So, can I take it from the frosty relations between the two of you that things are not going well on the wooing front?"

Hugh looked down at his empty cup. "I think I made a bit of a hash of things today, so yes things are not how I would like. I mentioned marriage and she said she would think about it."

Ewan winced. "Give yourself credit, dear brother. From the daggers that Mary is staring at you, I would suggest you have made a complete mess of things. But at least she didn't refuse you outright."

The mirth that he saw threatening on his brother's face did not help with Hugh's mood. "I am glad you find it amusing."

Ewan glanced over at Mary, then looked back. "I would hazard a guess that she is angry with you because you haven't gone about courting her in the right way, not because you asked her to marry you. You might want to question how you intend to woo her."

Standing on the side of Strathmore Mountain earlier that morning, Hugh had been blessed with the epiphany he so badly needed. If she was angry over the lack of romance he had shown during their encounter in the barn, it must have been because she expected him to woo her. And by wanting him to woo her, that meant she must feel something for him. He took that piece of insightful logic a step further —Mary being angry was actually a good thing.

Ewan gave him a brotherly pat on the shoulder and smiled. "Take heart from the knowledge that you are not the first of the Radley lads to have made a mess of their attempt to secure a wife. Now you just have to find a way to show her a different side of your relationship. One that takes things further than simply being friends, if you get my meaning?"

David's nursemaid came and took him from Mary. Ewan nodded as Caroline waved him over. "I shall see you in the morning."

Ewan escorted his wife from the room. Charles picked up a sleeping Will and led Adelaide and Lady Alison toward the stone steps, bidding everyone a good night as they departed.

Eventually only Hugh, Mary, and Aunt Maude were left. Aunt Maude was fast asleep in a high-backed chair in front of the fire, her hands resting gently in her lap.

Hugh decided it was time to make another attempt to speak to

Mary. He rose from his seat and came to stand in front of her. "May I join you?"

Mary looked up, then across to Aunt Maude.

Hugh followed her gaze. "Don't worry about Maude; she always falls asleep in front of the fire. She sleeps the sleep of the dead. Her maid and a footman will eventually come to escort her upstairs."

He needed time to talk to Mary, so he was happy to let sleeping aunts lie.

He took a seat on the sofa next to Mary. "I must apologize for this morning. It was thoughtless of me."

"Yes, it was. Perhaps we might be better off if we forget about it completely," she replied.

"No. I don't want us to forget about it. I want another chance. Give me the days until Hogmanay to show you what really does lie between us. If your answer after that is no then I will accept it," he said.

She looked at him, and he was dismayed to see sadness in her eyes. She wasn't angry with him; she was hurt.

He took hold of her hand, relieved when she did not pull away. "Please."

"Yes, Hugh. You have until New Year's Eve, but I am not sure if that will make any difference." Mary rose from the sofa. "I need to go to bed now. It's been a long day."

He followed her as she headed toward the steps which led up to the private family apartments. "Mary, wait," he said.

She stopped and turned. Hugh pointed to the mistletoe hanging overhead.

She shook her head. "I think we will need more than a little old-fashioned Christmas magic."

Hugh came to her side and leaned in to place a brief kiss on her cheek. "I am going to use all means at my disposal. If a little magic helps with my quest, then so be it."

Chapter Sixteen

Mary leaned back against the door of her bedroom and closed her eyes. She had taken a risk with Hugh and so far, it had worked. But to claim his heart, she knew she would have to hold her nerve steady.

Her fingertips touched the place on her cheek where he had kissed her. Two years and an unknown number of months she had waited for a kiss.

"It was a peck, but it's a start."

She had slyly watched him all evening, taking heart from his obvious discomfort at her holding him at arm's-length. While playing with David, she had seen Hugh speak to his brother. When Ewan ventured a look in her direction, their gazes met, and he had offered up the hint of a smile before turning back to Hugh. The Duke of Strathmore's silent approval gave her the encouragement she needed in order to stand her ground.

Hugh had asked for a few days to show her how well they would suit before expecting her answer to his proposal. She could only hope that he felt enough for her to be able to manage more than a small kiss on the cheek.

"Come on, Hugh, don't fail me. Don't fail us."

~

The following day had an unexpected start for Mary. No one had mentioned that most of the menfolk would be out on the mountain hunting wild boar for the better part of the day. Hugh had gone with the hunting party when it set out at first light and not returned until supper.

Mary had spent the day with the Radley women, making more juniper bundles. By the time supper came around, her aching fingers had her wishing never to see another bundle of juniper in her life.

It was late when Mary and Hugh finally got a moment alone. Everyone else, except Aunt Maude, had retired to bed. Maude was in her usual spot in front of the fire, fast asleep.

Hugh, seated in the chair opposite to Mary, was nursing a badly bruised leg from the hunt.

"What did you do exactly?" she asked, pointing at his leg.

He huffed. "Nothing heroic unfortunately. I tripped over a branch on the mountain and landed heavily. I don't know which is more bruised: my leg or my pride. The rest of the hunting party had a grand laugh when they saw me go head over heels into the heather."

"I could rub some comfrey cream into it if you like," she offered, trying not to laugh.

Hugh smiled warmly, reflecting the amusement she knew was on her own face. He rose from the chair and came to sit beside her.

An awkward silence settled between them for a moment before he finally spoke. "I know why I fell over this morning; I was busy thinking about you and not looking where I was going. To be honest, I have been thinking a lot about you since we left England."

He reached out and took hold of her hand. She shuddered as he raised it to his lips and kissed her palm. Their gazes met.

"My brother thinks you are in love with me. He says he has watched you and your eyes rarely leave me when we are in the same room. I thought he was mistaken, but I watched you tonight, and I think he might be right," he said.

"And?" Mary prayed his answer would be a swift one—if she held her breath for any longer, she may faint.

"And I need to know if you do feel something for me, because I have to tell you, my affections toward you are not those merely of a friend. They haven't been for some time," he said.

It was a good thing that they were seated away from the fireplace, as the whoosh of air which left her lungs would surely have threatened to put out the flames.

"You . . . you love me?" A trickle of a tear rolled down her cheek. The love she saw shining in his eyes threatened to bring on more tears.

"Yes, Mary, I do love you," he whispered. He speared his fingers into her hair and drew her to him, placing a searing kiss on her lips. The heady scent of his cologne, the same one she had gifted him, filled her senses.

Their tongues met in a soft dance. Every kiss he offered invited her to respond—to show her love for him. Mary was determined to hold nothing back.

Aunt Maude stirred in her chair.

They released one another from the kiss and sat with their foreheads touching while they both regained their breath.

A shy smile sat on Mary's face. "I love you, Hugh. I always have."

He took hold of her hands. "I was a fool not to have spoken my heart to you a long time ago. I promise I won't ever hold my love from you again."

Aunt Maude grumbled in her sleep and yawned.

Hugh cast his eye in her direction, then looked back at Mary.

"Come with me." He took her by the hand and led her toward the steps. When they arrived under the mistletoe, he stopped.

Mary waited, expecting another soft, chaste kiss on the cheek.

"We don't need magic, but I think we should still avail ourselves of it just to be sure." He let out a growl before pulling her to him, swiftly taking her lips in another kiss which was anything but chaste. She clung to him as he plundered her mouth, meeting his hungry need with her own.

When he finally released her from the kiss, he held her close. His eyes burned bright with desire—desire she knew was for her.

"I can walk you to your room and we can say good night, or you can come with me and we can greet the dawn together. Either way, we will be making an announcement tomorrow morning," he said, his voice gruff with barely restrained passion.

Mary nodded. "The dawn sounds perfect." She placed her hand in his and they walked from the great hall.

As they disappeared up the steps, Lady Maude Radley rose from her chair. She crossed to the sofa where Hugh and Mary had been sitting. From behind one of the cushions, she retrieved a sprig of mistletoe. She held it up and softly chuckled.

"Old-fashioned Christmas magic always goes a long way."

Chapter Seventeen

Hugh and Mary stole into his private apartment, and Hugh locked the door behind them. He pulled her into his embrace again and kissed her with the urgency and passion she sensed he had barely held in check back in the great hall.

"Are you sure you want to be here with me tonight? I will understand if you wish to wait," he said.

Matters between them were moving fast but Mary had lain awake too many nights, imaging what she would do if she was ever given the chance to lie with Hugh, to even consider holding back at this pivotal moment.

Laying her hands on his stubbled cheeks, she drew him to her, and placed tender, inviting kisses on his lips. "I have waited long enough for you, Lord Hugh Radley. Tonight, you become mine."

"And you mine. But first thing's first," he said, releasing her hands.

Hugh crossed to the tallboy which sat in the corner of his room and opened the top drawer. Mary took a deep breath and prayed that if this was indeed a dream, she would never wake from it.

He returned, stealing a warm kiss from her.

"We have to do this properly," he said. With her hand held in his, he went down on bended knee. "I can be blind to some things at times;

it is a fault in my nature. But my love for you has always been there, and always will be. You know my shortcomings better than anyone. And as my partner in this life, I empower you to take me to task if you ever feel that I am being anything less than fully supportive of you," he said.

With a wry grin, Mary nodded. "I shall hold you to that, Hugh Radley."

"Good. Mary Margaret Gray, I love you and want to spend the rest of my life with you. Will you do me the greatest honor possible and become my wife?"

There were a dozen other words she could have used at that moment, including *finally* and *about time*, but her heart was so full of love for the man who knelt before her that Mary could only think of one. "*Yes*."

He got to his feet and slipped a diamond ring on her finger. The oval-shaped stone was set in gold with a delicate filigree pattern etched into it. It was perfect in its elegance and simplicity. Hugh knew her better than she realized.

"Edinburgh has some fine jewelers as well as clothing stores," he whispered.

"Oh, Hugh."

And she had thought he'd only been worried about keeping her warm. The wicked man had been planning to ask her to marry him all along.

She looked down at the ring and sighed. "This is the most beautiful Christmas gift anyone could ever receive. Thank you."

Hugh slipped his hand around her waist. "The ring is a betrothal gift, my love. I have something else planned for my fiancée for Christmas Day, but you will have to wait."

He was the most handsome, wonderful, and at times infuriating man she had ever met, but she would not have exchanged him for anyone else. Hugh Radley was exactly the man for her.

She wiped away a tear, then, emboldened by his declaration of love, she stole one kiss. Then another. By the time she was ready for a third touch of his lips, Hugh had tightened his grip about her waist and pulled her hard against him. His low growl of need set her heart racing.

Until now, her private fantasies of this moment had been enough to keep her satisfied. With his heated touch, her desire raced to a dangerous level.

He stepped back from her, and with what she imagined was an unintended overly dramatic flourish, tore his scarf from his neck. With the mixture of nerves and the humor of his look, she snorted a laugh. He raised an eyebrow in her direction as he tossed the scarf on a nearby sofa. His jacket quickly followed.

"Your turn," he murmured.

Mary looked at Hugh's clothes laying in a pile. Seeing them now brought home the reality of the situation. She was tempted to pinch herself; this was really happening. Never had she dared to imagine that her secret dreams of being with him would come to fruition. Now they were.

A worried look appeared on his face when she didn't move. For her, this moment was more than a simple physical encounter. Her love for him ran to her very soul.

She held out a hand and was reassured when he took it and drew himself closer once more. "Hugh," she murmured, offering up her mouth to his. He nipped at her bottom lip, teasing. She nipped him back, her breath shuddering.

No longer needing any invitation, she placed her hands on his face, drawing him down to her. Their mouths locked in a fiery embrace, tongues tangled. It was a wicked dance.

When she finally released him from the kiss, Mary knew the time had come. Time for her to follow his lead.

With a deft shrug, she let her wool shawl fall to the floor. She resisted the temptation to follow Hugh's example and toss it away. She had a terrible throwing arm and the shawl was more likely to end up in the fireplace than on the sofa. She kicked it safely aside.

After sliding a finger under the top of her gown sleeve, she pulled it down. Her intention of revealing a hint of shoulder failed miserably in the attempt. The sleeve wouldn't budge. She silently rued the sensible nature of Scottish clothing. They both chuck

"You may have to help me with the fastenings," she said.

He turned her to face away from him, then began to undo the ties on the back of her gown. For every knot he untied, he placed a kiss on the nape of her neck. Mary shivered with anticipation.

"For my sake, you might want to have a word with your maid about how tight she ties these laces. This could take a while."

When she was finally free of her binds, Mary stepped out of her gown. Hugh rewarded her with yet another kiss.

His shirt was next to go. Mary made quick work of the button at the top and watched with bated breath as she got her first glimpse of his hair-dusted chest.

She lay a hand over his heart, feeling its steady beat. A heart she knew beat for her. "You are the most . . ."

He brushed a hand on her cheek as she stood, lost for words. Hugh lifted his shirt free from the top of his kilt and pulled it over his head.

With his bare torso and striking blue and gray kilt, he looked for all the world like a rugged Scottish highlander—one she was hoping would soon ravish her. He took hold of the buckle of his belt and gave her another saucy grin.

He took his hand away and she mewed with disappointment. Her elusive prize remained hidden under layers of heavy wool. When he met her eyes, she saw all humor had disappeared from his face.

"I want you to do this; that way, you are in control. Nothing happens from this moment on without your express permission," he said.

She lay her trembling fingers on the buckle of his belt. His words were perfect in their reverence. They would have a lifetime of knowing each another, but there would only ever be one first time. A moment to treasure always.

She looked deep into his piercing blue eyes as she separated the leather belt from the buckle and dropped it to the floor. His kilt quickly followed.

Her gaze drifted lower, taking in the sight of Hugh in all his splendor. She sucked in a hesitant breath. She knew enough from overhearing the not-so-scholarly discussions in the meals hall at college to understand the state of his manhood and what it meant.

He wanted her.

"May I?" he asked, taking hold of the sides of her shift.

"Please."

As her shift joined the rest of the scattered garments on the floor, Mary resisted the instinctive reaction to cover herself. She was about to become his woman; this moment demanded full honesty between them. She let her hands fall to her sides.

"Come," he said, offering her his hand.

Hugh drew her to the bed and pulled back the covers before laying her down on the soft linen sheets. He soon joined her, rolling over so that they faced one another. She shivered as he reached out and cupped one of her breasts. Her whole world tilted as Hugh bent his head and, drawing a nipple into his mouth, gently nipped at it with his teeth.

"Oh, my sweet . . ." she murmured.

She clutched at the bedclothes as he slipped a finger into her heat and began to stroke. He sucked hard on her nipple, and Mary whimpered. The torture was exquisite.

When he finally released her nipple from his masterful attention, he rose over her, and gave her a kiss that made her toes curl.

She groaned as he slipped a second finger into her, and when his thumb began to rub against her sensitive bud, she sobbed. Her need for release built with every stroke.

"Is that good? Tell me if you want me to change anything. I can go harder or deeper; I am at your command," he said.

"Don't stop," Mary pleaded.

"I love you," he said.

She was beyond words at this moment, unable to reciprocate his declaration, consumed by the driving need to find her sexual release.

He slowed his strokes and murmured in her ear. "I want you come, but I need to be inside you when you do."

She opened her eyes as he released her from his touch. He moved between her legs, his hard erection brushing the side of her inner thigh.

"This may sting for a second, but I need you to stay with me. As soon as your body accepts me, I will make it enjoyable again," he said.

Placing the bulk of his weight on one arm, he lowered himself over her before slowly parting her slick folds with his cock. Mary winced at the sensation of Hugh stretching her and held her breath.

He stilled, patiently waiting for her body to adjust. The discomfort eased and she slowly breathed out.

"Does it still hurt?"

"No," she replied.

He began to move within her, slowly at first then quickening as his strokes deepened. With her hands gripping either side of his hips, she urged him on. The tension began to build within her once more. Her need to reach the peak came with every one of his thrusts. His groans of pleasure added to her own.

She crashed through on the end of one of his deep and powerful thrusts, sobbing his name as she came. Hugh buried his face into the base of her neck. She felt the nip of his teeth on her skin before he let out a shout. He shuddered, then collapsed on top of her, pressing her into the mattress.

Mary wrapped her arms and legs around him and held him to her, promising to herself that she would never let this man go.

Chapter Eighteen

"**I**s that everything?"

Hugh looked inside the basket Mary held in her hands, pointing at each of the items. "Bread, blackbun, and salt for food. A bottle of whisky for your host's good health... Oh, I forgot the coin." He opened his sporran and pulled out a gold coin. "This is for wealth. This is a pistole; the last of the coins minted for Scotland."

He dropped it into the basket, stealing a kiss from his wife in the process. "Now you are ready."

The love she saw shining in his eyes was the same she had beheld on Christmas Eve as she and Hugh had stood facing one another to speak their marriage vows in the castle chapel. Ewan had escorted her down the aisle to the tune of a single bagpipe, beaming as he placed her hand in Hugh's.

The Radley family had, of course, been delighted when a sheepish Hugh and Mary appeared at breakfast the morning after spending their first night together and announced their betrothal. Master Crowdie had overseen a flurry of activity in the castle and village, which saw Hugh and Mary married that same day.

Aunt Maude gave the bride a family heirloom wedding band, which matched Mary's engagement ring to perfection. The Duchess and

Dowager Duchess of Strathmore presented Mary with a blue woolen gown and a matching Strathmore tartan sash and shawl. Mary Radley was now one of the family.

It was New Year's Eve, Hogmanay in Scotland, and in a break with tradition, Mary had been chosen to conduct the ancient First Foot ceremony.

Earlier in the evening, she and Hugh had led the castle staff down to the village and shared a hot supper with them. Her welcome into the Strathmore Castle and village family had been so heartfelt that she'd felt close to tears at many moments during the day. Only Hugh's constant presence—he was never far from her—kept her from dissolving into a weeping mess.

Master Crowdie strode into the village tavern with a large brass bell in his hand. A hush fell over the gathering before he swung the bell high and rang it loudly. He then turned and marched out the door.

Hugh offered Mary his arm and they followed. A happy, chatting group of villagers took up the rear. Flaming torches held on spikes were dotted along the road to light the way back to the castle.

Walking arm in arm with her husband, Mary felt sure of her future, and thanks to her trusty tackety boots, also of her footing. Her Strathmore tartan shawl kept the bitter night wind at bay.

As they crossed over the drawbridge and into the castle bailey, a loud cheer rose from the assembly. Hugh smiled at her. "The cheers are for you, my love."

They waited until everyone from the village had arrived and gathered around them in the courtyard. Master Crowdie pulled out his pocket watch and checked it. He nodded toward Mary. Hugh let go of her arm and stood back, a huge smile of pride on his face.

She gave him one last nervous look, then climbed the steps of the keep. A hush descended on the crowd. All eyes were fixed on Master Crowdie.

He held his hand up and then dropped it to his side. The bells in the village church began to peal. The castle chapel bell rang in time. The crowd looked to where Mary stood on the steps of the castle keep.

She took hold of the door knocker and raised it before hitting it hard on the wood. The knock echoed in the still night air.

She did it a second time, and then a third.

After the third knock, the door of the keep slowly opened. Ewan Radley stood in the doorway, a glass of whisky in his hand.

Mary cleared her throat. "A happy new year and good tidings to you and yours," she said.

She handed him the basket, and Ewan gave her the glass of whisky in exchange. He stepped back and she crossed the threshold. Inside the great hall, all the Radley family, her family, were gathered. The heady scent of burnt juniper filled her nostrils.

Ewan shrugged. "Evil spirits only leave if you burn enough juniper to have everyone's eyes watering."

At the sound of steps on the stone flagging behind her, she turned and saw Hugh race in the door, just ahead of the rest of the castle staff and villagers. He grabbed hold of the door and after swinging it fully open, stood and held it for the crowd which quickly filed through.

The great hall was filled with lit torches, and on the first table was a mass of cups—all full of whisky from the look of it. One by one, the villagers took up a cup. Then, with their whisky untouched, they stood back and waited.

When every last cup of whisky had been taken, Ewan Radley climbed up on one of the roughly hewn wooden tables. Master Crowdie held up his hand once more. Silence descended on the great hall.

The Duke of Strathmore was about to speak.

Chapter Nineteen

❧❀❧

"**W**ylcome to you all, this most special of days. May the new year find you blessed by good fortune and good health," he said.

Some of the younger members of the gathering went to raise their cups to drink, but a growl from Master Crowdie had those same cups quickly lowered.

Ewan shook his head, a smile still on his lips. "Now some of you may have noticed that our First Foot tonight was indeed a woman. But she is of dark hair and also a member of the Radley family, so I think the sprits of Hogmanay will forgive my trespass," he said.

Hugh caught a sideways glance at his new bride. Mary's eyes shone bright with happiness. The touch of her fingers met his, and he leaned in and brushed a soft kiss on her cheek. A soft "ah" rippled through the gathering.

"I see I am going to have to make this a short speech," Ewan added, looking directly at his brother.

Hugh grinned back at him. He was a newlywed, and that entitled him to a healthy degree of leeway.

"As I was saying, my family and I welcome you all to our home tonight. And to Mary, a special welcome on the occasion of not only your first Hogmanay, but your first as my brother Hugh's wife. Thank you for your First Foot gifts; we shall put them to good use. To the rest of the Strathmore family, I am both honored and humbled to serve as your laird. I raise my glass to you and yours. May the new year be a good one and your health stay hearty. *Slainte!*"

"*Slainte!*"

The sound of cups and glasses being clinked together echoed through the great hall, followed by loud cheers of "Happy New Year!"

With the formalities over, Hugh pulled Mary into his arms and gave her the kiss he had been aching to give to her all evening. Her soft lips met his as she melted into his embrace. Holding her in his arms was as natural as breathing

"Happy New Year, Husband," she said.

"Happy New Year, my wife, my love," said Hugh.

Waking up beside her that morning had been a gift beyond words. He'd been humbled when she had welcomed him into her arms, and they'd made love. With the new year would come a new life for the both of them. Knowing that every day he would be blessed with her love had him lost for words.

"Come," she said.

He let her lead him over to where the mistletoe still hung.

"I love you," she said, wrapping her arms around his neck.

Hugh did the only thing a newlywed man could do. He pulled his wife into his arms and, ignoring the cheers of the crowd, kissed her senseless.

With his loving wife to support him, Hugh Radley did make a success of his career in the Church of England, rising to one of its highest positions of rank, eventually becoming the Bishop of London.

And every year he, along with Mary and their children, would arrive at Strathmore Castle a few days before Christmas, bringing with them a red box.

Inside that box would be a perfect branch of mistletoe, ready to weave its magic.

Also by Sasha Cottman

The Duke of Strathmore

Letter from a Rake (ebook, print, audio)

An Unsuitable Match (ebook, print, audio)

The Duke's Daughter (ebook, print, audio)

A Scottish Duke for Christmas (ebook, print)

My Gentleman Spy (ebook, print, audio)

Lord of Mischief (ebook, print, audio)

The Ice Queen (ebook, print, audio)

Two of a Kind (ebook, print, audio)

Mistletoe & Kisses (ebook, print)

Regency Rockstars

Reid (ebook, print)

Owen (ebook, print)

Callum (ebook, print)

Kendal (ebook, print)

London Lords

An Italian Count for Christmas (ebook, print)

About the Author

USA Today bestselling author Sasha Cottman was born in England, but raised in Australia. Having her heart in two places has created a love for travel, which at last count was to over 55 countries. A travel guide is always on her pile of new books to read.

Sasha's novels are set around the Regency period in England, Scotland, and Europe. Her books are centred on the themes of love, honour, and family.

For your FREE ebook of A Wild English Rose and details of Sasha's latest releases visit her website at www.sashacottman.com

Printed in Great Britain
by Amazon

81155154R00058